# About the Author

It is the very first novel of Kartik Srivastava. He was born in the Manchester city, Kanpur of the state, Uttar Pradesh. After finishing his class X from highly renowned Mercy Memorial School, he changed his school and completed his class XII from Harmilap Mission School. Now he is the student of B.tech 3rd year from Raj Kumar Goel Engineering College, Ghaziabad. He is presently living in Ghaziabad.

Kartik loves to play guitar in his free time. Besides being a writer, he is a good poet also. Some of his written poems can be viewed on his blog Kartiksrivastava.blogspot.in.

The best way to contact Kartik Srivastava is through his novel's page on Facebook. You can also write to him at transkartik@gmail.com.

# The Promise of Love

## Kept Alive

Kartik Srivastava

PARTRIDGE
A Penguin Random House Company

**To order additional copies of this book, contact**
Partridge India
000 800 10062 62
orders.india@partridgepublishing.com

www.partridgepublishing.com/india

To

# The *Aafat Girl* of my life.
*(I Will Always Miss You)*


*Tere naa hone se bas itni kami hai,*
*Mai laakh muskuraaun fir bhi,*
*In aankhon me nami hai....*

- Anonymous

# Acknowledgement

Writing the acknowledgement is the most difficult part of the whole book. You always have a fear in mind that some name might get left behind.

Well, since this is my first book, therefore I won't lie. (*It doesn't mean that I will lie in my second book. Hahaha!*) I would like to thank each and every person who helped me survive the birthing of this book. Without their sincere efforts, I would never have accomplished it.

Oh, yes, the list can be long enough.

I would first of all like to thank my readers, who purchased this book and encouraged a budding writer to write more.

I am highly grateful to all my sisters, especially my eldest sister, **Tripti Srivastava** and her friend **Nisha Mukesh,** who sparked the idea of writing a book, merely by noticing few of my poems. I am thankful to **Tripti Srivastava** for being a support at every step of this journey of mine, whether it be getting the print outs or getting them arrange in a presentable manner. I am thankful to her for suggesting me the different ideas about the story and supervising my work regularly. I am also thankful to her for allowing me to use her laptop. Hahaha!

I would really say that this was going to be a never ending process until one of my close friends, **Shivangi Sharma**, who took interest in my work and always comforted me with her kind words. She always cheered me up. I would like to thank her for reading the whole book and suggesting me with the corrections. Love you for that, girl!

Now I would like to thank my other sisters- **Deepti Srivastava, Tulika Srivastava, Mallika Srivastava, Kritika Srivastava,** for keeping it secret from my mom and dad. Hahaha!

I am highly grateful to my younger sister **Kritika Srivastava,** for keeping that secret when it was required because she cannot digest any secrets. Hahaha!

**Arun Chaturvedi,** it would never have been possible for me to write without your help. Thanks for guiding me and always boosting me up with his words, '*Tu likh bhai, teri book zarur market me aayegi*'. You were always available for me whenever I needed any help regarding it.

I would really have got lost in my own book had it not been for **Ananya Neogi,** my cute, sweet and bestest friend, who found me every time. I always mailed her every single chapter whenever I finished it. She used to take some precious time out of her busy schedule and read those irritating and frustrating chapters. I am very very thankful to her for never having expressed her annoyance; instead she used to edit it with some really nice lines, as beautiful as she herself is. I am in your debt *Doraemon*!

I would have broken down a long way back, if **Abhishek Verma** had not been there with me. He was always a call away. He supported me with his presence. He used to come along with me wherever I had to go for my book, whether it is the Copyright Office or anywhere, he was always a helping hand. Love you brother!

My batch mates, **Dinesh Nigam, Kartikay Verma, Ashutosh Yadav, Ajeet Singh, Gautam Kumar, Anuj Sharma, Akhilesh Kushwaha, and Arun Chaturvedi.** I will be always thankful to them for providing me with proxies in every other lecture. Because of them my attendance was satisfactory and the H.O.D never called up my parents.

Now it would come down to **Chetna Nema** and **Shubhanshi Mishra,** my college friends, who were happier than me for my book. I cannot tell how lucky I am to find these two girls. They would always say, *'I am eagerly waiting for the book to be out and I am very happy for the book'.* Many thanks to them for trusting in my work and this is for you, **Shubhanshi,** you always asked whether you will like this book or not as you are not in love. So, I would love to share a thought which will answer your question, *'To enjoy a love story, it is never necessary to be in love. Let's be honest, sometimes reading the love story of others can be the most calming thing in this world'.*

Now I would write down the name of **Kashish Garg,** a girl whom I met in a train journey and she became a very good friend of mine. I would thank her for suggesting me the name of the girl in lead.

**Garvit Gupta, Nikhil Yadav, Sankalp Srivastava, Shubham Lath, Shobhita Ghai, Shivangi Gupta, Swapnil Srivastava, Nikhil Gupta, Rohit Kumar, Rajdeep Singh, Ragini Kapoor** and **Aarohy Kapoor,** who thought it was a joke till they realized the seriousness of it. They might be joking but I would like to thank all of them for always comforting me with their words, *'It will be a national best-seller'*. Of course, no one read the manuscript!

It would not have been possible without the support of my two friends-cum-brother, **Arvind Pandey** and **Aman Singh.**

**Sheshan Singh,** for all the motivation, without which this would not have been possible.

I would like to thank **Shukrati Singh,** a friend, a sister and a beautiful person for teasing me about the book all the time.

**Manas Bhatia,** a writer like me and above all, he is a dear friend. He encouraged me to complete the story. I would like to thank him for being supporting me with his messages. He is also writing a novel which is in its finishing stage and when I got to know this, I took a sigh of relief. I thought that there are people who are like you. I wish you a good luck for your first novel dude!

How can I forget to mention the name of that one person who was the key to the book, **Deepita Bhatnagar,** my **closest** and **dearest** friend. I am sincerely thankful to her as without her, I would never have come up with any story. She is the inspiration. Also, I would like to thank her for suggesting me a different and a better end for the story. It was the distance and longing that made this all possible. The more I wrote, the more those miles disappeared. Truly, I never had a friend like you in my life whom I can miss even after so many years of *misfortune*. Thanks for letting me miss you. I wish that someday these miles between us will fully disappear and we will be back together. Thanks for everything!

Now I want to thanks **my parents** for believing in me and supporting me both, emotionally and financially. Also, I would thank them for sending me to the IIT-JEE coaching, well that's got a lot to contribute here. Also, I met the leading lady of this book, there only, so Mom and Dad, a big thank you to both of you. Love you Mom and Dad! Okay! Dad, but I have some issues with you, hahaha, and no serious ones though! You know what I mean!

Last but not the least; I am highly obliged to **Partridge Publishers,** my publisher for providing me with an opportunity such as this. Also, I would like to thank them for believing in me. I would also like to thank my friend **Ketan Mishra** who not only read my book thoroughly and patiently but also corrected many of the mistakes. Again I would like to thank him for correcting even the smallest mistake in my book. It is because of him that this book is so much more beautiful than I thought it would ever be.

Now, I think the list is complete and if I missed few names then apologies for that. I am extremely sorry if I forgot to mention anybody's name who worked equally hard, willingly or unwillingly, as I did for this book.

Thank you everyone!
Love you all.
Always-
Kartik

# Introduction

Love - Have you ever wondered, what really this word means? Is it just a word or more than it? Is it just affection or something more? No one knows the answer to these questions. They just say, they understand the meaning of love but do they? I doubt it.

Now, answer one more question to yourself, what is a TRUE Love? You will think of the person whom you love the most in this world. So, are there any conditions and promises in this so called true love? I think it would be slightly unfair to answer it. Some of you will say yes, and some will be against it.

What if you are bound by certain promises and conditions in love? Now think, what if these very same promises that we so solemnly keep prove to be the death of us? Then will you blame the promises or the people who made them? What is the need of those promises when they cannot guarantee happiness in your relation even when one keeps them? Who is to be blamed, the one who keeps them or the one who made them?

Does true love actually need them? This is the question, which must be haunting many of you.

You may think that, how can a true love need promises? If it needs, then is it really a true love? It is not that the two people don't have faith on each other, in fact, it is the feeling of insecurity of losing him/her. Promises are the result of over affection.

Above all, what could be the worst result of loving each other truly?

Is it joy or sorrow?

Is it worth it?

Well, we will find the answers to all these questions in the end.

It is just a friendly advice to all my readers, who are in a relationship to trust your partner and love with all your heart and soul. Do not make fun of this divine word – LOVE. It is difficult to find a true partner, but, once you find, don't let them go.

Be truthful and enjoy the lovely time. There is nothing in this world which can match the power of love.

If you fight, then try to solve out ASAP! You never know when this might turn out to be your last fight! Who knows what life has to offer you tomorrow? It is quite possible that you may regret it your whole life.

So, stop fighting, start loving. Fall in love, celebrate love, cherish it, enjoy it, love it. Being in love is the most beautiful feeling one can ever have.

To all the boys – be gentle, don't be rude on her. You never know how much she loves you. You never know what she gives up to be with you. Handle her with care! She is not only for having a lovely company but also to be pampered and taken care of. It is not easy being a girl. Thank her for even the stupidest thing she does for you because love is just a huge collection of these small and stupid moments.

To all the girls – never think, he doesn't love you as much as you do. He may never show but his eyes will betray the emotions underneath. Try to understand him, at times, he only needs you. He is not there only to go out shopping with you but also to be heard, even though he is perfectly silent!

Guys just enhance your love and blossom it. It is an unbearable pain when it is over. Never let it happen.

My good wishes are with all of you. May god bless you all! May you never face separation!

Now, I must request my dear readers, for the sake of love, just think of the person you have ever loved with all your heart and soul.

I hope that after you finish reading this book, many of you will change your views for the word 'Love' and also many of you will find a new meaning to the word 'True Love'.

This story, it might not really exist, but it is there in my heart, and that's true enough.

Is it my story? I don't know.

Is it a fiction? Quite a possibility.

Is it inspired from a true story? Absolutely.

But whose? Let's find out.

# Chapter One

September 29, 2013:

Dusk had fallen. It was a typical September night. The black canvas of the night sky was decorated with twinkling stars. Moon was tucked to its corner. A grand celebration was planned by the Maathur family for that auspicious night. The night was as beautiful as the reason of that grand celebration. Many relatives were present at the place. It was decorated with flowers and appeared to be bathed in light. While many of them shared the cause behind celebration, many were simply there for the sake of it.

It appeared as if whole of the Lucknow city had been present there, that night.

Mishti could not understand. She felt out of place.

'Take care of the guests' her father ordered the servants.

'Where is Mishti?' her maasi queried.

'Must be in her room' replied her cousin running towards the kitchen.

'Is she alright?' asked her doctor, 'Does she remember anything?'

'Did she ask about Kavya, yet?' asked her maasi.

'She asked yesterday but we changed the topic. Is it safe to tell her the truth?' her mother asked the doctor.

'I think, this is not the right time. She has just recovered from such a trauma'

'But one day, we will have to tell her'

'That day is not today, not tomorrow. It is not the time. Let her recover fully'

'You are right but how long can we avoid her questions?'

'As long as it is possible'

Mishti was still in her room, wondering about the party and thinking about Kavya. She was happy to see her family so happy but at the same time her mind was occupied with Kavya.

Having no idea about the party with everyone apparently too busy to tell her anything, she sat undecided in her room.

'Where is he? Is he in the party downstairs? Should I call him? What is the party about? She asked these questions to herself but could answer only one of them.

She picked her phone and dialled his number. The number was out of service. Her heart sank. Then a question hit her mind which actually left her dumbstruck.

She suddenly looked around anxiously for the calendar. It was 2013! Her phone confirmed it. But that wasn't possible, it had to be 2012.

For a moment she sat too baffled to move. She focused hard but all her efforts went in vain. She straight away ran downstairs to her mother.

'Where is Kavya? What happened to me? Is he okay? Is he here? Why does the calendar show 2013?'

Her mother didn't know what to answer.

'Relax beta. Enjoy the party.' All she could manage.

She threw up her hands in anguish and looked around utterly confused and anxious. 'What the hell is going on?'

'Okay, I will answer all your questions after the party'

She wanted to scream out, 'What party?', but resisted. Her teeth shut tight and with all the effort her patience required she said,

'Fair enough'

There were tears in her eyes. Tears of desperation and premonitions.

She waited desperately for the party to get over. Meanwhile she was occupied with her brother who tried to calm her down.

'What happened, bhaiya?'

'Nothing, everything is fine'

'There is something that you all are hiding from me'

'Absolutely not beta'

She shot him a sarcastic look and went in her room.

It was a little late when the party finally got over. Now there were only she and her family.

'Now, tell me the truth'

'What truth?' asked her father.

'That where is Kavya? You said he will be in the party but he didn't show up'

'Must be busy with his work' her brother replied.

'And also it is not easy to come from Kanpur, just for a small party' her maasi replied.

'Small! It looks quite a grand party to me. And what was the reason for it?

Everyone looked each other in search of an answer when she asked again, 'Where is he? What happened? And why the hell is it 2013?'

She started to shout and her mother broke down.

'Stop. For god sake, please stop stressing yourself. I can't lose you again'

'Again! What do you mean by that?'

'N-n-n-o-t-h-i-n-g'

'Please tell me, I beg all of you' she cried this time.

Her tears melted down everyone and finally the doctor had to intervene to the conversation.

'We are sorry that we hid this from you but believe us you are not in a mental state to receive this'

'I want my answers. That's it' she shouted at the top of her voice.

'Okay! You don't remember anything because you were been sleeping for 554 days that means you were in coma'

The ground beneath her feet escaped. She stood motionless. Her heartbeat increased and she was not able to believe what she had just heard. Before she could ask about the confirmation, her mother said, 'Yes dear, you opened your eyes yesterday only'

'B-b-u-t where is Kavya? The last thing I remember was being with him' Hazy images of a steering wheel and a road flashed in her mind. She pressed her fingers to her temple as pain hit her head.

'He must be perfectly okay. We owe a lot to him' her father replied.

These answers somehow satisfied her but she was still worried about Kavya. Everyone was quiet on the matter of Kavya so she decided to find the answers, herself.

She collected the facts that she knew about him like his address, his father's name and similar more facts. She only remembered the days before March 22, 2012. She then dialled the number of Kanika, her friend and Kavya's sister.

Kanika was working on her college project in her home when she received a call from her number. She was over joyous and shocked to see her name on the mobile screen.

'Hello! Mishti, is it you?'

'Yes, Kanika...'

'What!! Oh my god! You recovered from coma? This is very very great. I am so so happy.' She interrupted Mishti.

'It's good to listen to your voice dear. I missed you so much. I can't explain what I went through' Mishti started crying and so did Kanika.

'Where is Kavya? His number is not reachable'

'What? Are you serious Mishti?'

'What do you mean? What happened?'

'Nothing. Leave all that and tell me when are you coming Kanpur to meet? I am dying to meet you now'

'Me too. I need a tight hug from you yaar. I will come soon'

'Okay. Take care and rest properly. Bye'

'Bye'

# Chapter Two

Few weeks later, Mishti went to Kanpur. She was received by Kanika. They both went home and the first thing they did was, they hugged each other tightly and cried out of happiness. They chatted for a long time. Few hours later, her mother came home who was out for shopping at the grocery store. She could not believe what she just saw but Mishti was actually standing in front of her. She just hugged her. Her watery eyes said a lot.

'Are you okay now, beta? Asked his mom.

'I will be, aunty'

'Yes, you both carry on; I'll get some snacks'

'Ji aunty'

'So Mishti, how are you feeling? I mean, quite disturbed or surprised?' asked Kanika.

'How will you feel one you will realise that you woke up after an year? But I am disturbed'

'Its ok, everything is perfectly alright now' *'I hope so' murmured* Kanika.

'What? Did you say anything?'

'No..no...no. So what are you planning next? I mean that you will be joining the college from next session?'

'Yes, I am planning to do it. This is the only option left. By the way, where is Kavya? In which college is he? Is he in Kanpur or somewhere else? When will he come?'

Kanika was in the middle of nowhere. She was thinking of changing the topic when God heard her silent prayers.

'Here girls, iced tea for both my girls'

'Thanks mom'

'Thanks Aunty'

Kanika gestured something to her mom and she understood.

'So, beta, you will be here for how many days?'

'Ummm... I guess aunty, for 3-4 days'

'Oh! It's good that you will be staying with us after a long gap'

'Actually aunty, I will come here again at the last day of me in Kanpur. I will be staying at my maasi's place.'

'Okay Okay.. but you have to come here the day before you leave'

'Okay, now I must leave, Maasi must be waiting'

Kanika accompanied her to her maasi's home and then returned back.

Next day when Kanika returned from college, she heard her parents talking about Mishti. She also joined the conversation.

'But it is totally wrong and unjust' she said.

'We are left with no choice' her father said.

'Moreover, time will make her forget everything. As time will pass, she will become normal and there is quite a possibility that she will forget us also' he added.

'But it will happen only when we will tell her the truth. There must be a thing to be forgotten. If she doesn't know anything then what will she forget?' Her mother said in a worried voice.

'I agree, but if her parents have not told her anything then why should we?' asked Kanika.

'Because, she came here with a hope to know some answers. I will suggest that we should tell her now. If we don't then there is no chance of her, forgetting this topic.'

'Mom, why are you so interested in telling her everything? Asked Kanika.

'It is because, she is like my daughter. She is the love of my son. She also loves him and I can't see her in this condition'

'Well, okay then. Do whatever you people want. Don't involve me, I have a lot of college work' Kanika said and went towards her room.

'Will it be okay? Will it be in control?' asked Kanika's father.

'I don't know but we have to take the chance. She had gone through many bad things and now if we don't tell her then it will be the worst thing to her.' Mom replied.

After a long discussion, they finally ended up on nothing.

As decided, Mishti came to the Srivastava's place. It was late in the afternoon. Kanika was in her college and her father was in his office. She was all alone with Kanika's mom. After chatting for a long time, Mishti asked the same question and this time she actually broke down.

It was like when a person searches for something and he always meets with lies, illusions but not the actual thing.

'Aunty, Where is he? Why aren't you guys telling me the truth?'

'Who he?'

'Kavya. where is he? Neither my family told me anything nor did you tell me anything. Are you not having pity on me? I have lost all my hope now. For god sake, please tell me everything.' She cried in front of her.

She tried to console her but she couldn't. Finally she gave up and said, 'Okay, don't cry beta. You are very close to him and I don't want to see you like this. Come with me'

She took her to Kavya's room. She very quietly opened his room. Everything was well placed. All the books were arranged properly. The bedding was perfect. The walls were neatly finished and were decorated with his pictures.

'Aunty, why you brought me here?'

'So that you can satisfy yourself'

'How? I will not be satisfied until and unless I see him. And why is his room so tidy? He never liked this. He has always loved his untidy room. Did he said for all this or he did himself? She asked very fluently.

'I'll leave you here now. Stay here for as long as you want.

Now it was Mishti and Kavya's room. She wondered why aunty said so and left.

She explored the room and found many things like his guitar, his photo collage, his trophies, their pictures. But nothing was so important. After spending at least two hours, she was just about to step out of the room when she noticed a blue diary.

It was designed with a guitar and was titled- 'Me and my memories - Sweet and bitter'.

She took it and called his mom.

'Aunty, what is this diary?'

'Oh, it is nothing. Kavya has just grown a habit of writing a diary after her tenth boards exams. Don't you know?'

'No, he never told me. What has he written?'

'I don't know. Must be about his friends and school. I never read it.'

'Okay, but if you allow then can I read this?' she asked for her permission.

'Of course you can. Permission granted. Now the truth is....'

'I didn't know that Mr. Kavya is a writer that he wrote a whole diary. Hahaha! It is funny. Okay, I'll read it'

Noticing that this diary of his brought a smile on her face, she stopped and left her alone with his diary.

Mishti took it in her hands, adjusted her position on the bed and opened the first page.

**(Now from the next chapter, let us read his diary along with Mishti.)**

# Chapter Three

It is a bright sunny day of the month of April, the sun is shining as if it has decided to shower fire today, sky is so blue and the white clouds appear to be hanging in the sky which could fall anytime. A hot yet not hot wind is slapping the face again and again. Trees are waiving like they have lost their minds, leaves are so green, all the weather seems to be very happy or maybe it is the same as everyday but today I see it differently. Today after so many days I am enjoying because I've just crossed my life's first hurdle; that is the 'Tenth class board exams'. I am very sure to get above 90% marks. Today, I've no tension in my mind and I am just enjoying these vacations with my heart buddies- Kshitij, Abhishek, Sahil, Lavanya, and Himani.

Let me first introduce you to the backbones of my life, as I mentioned their name above, now let me throw some more light on the special ones. First I'll paint the face of my 'chuddhy buddy'- **Kshitij Gupta**, what to say about this boy, he is one of the most humble persons I've ever met in my life. He is a multi-talented person, a musician, an artist; he is very good on guitar and keyboard and is also a good singer. He loves plants and animals and is a gadget-freak. He loves machines and enjoys driving car and is a passionate lover of them too. He is a good friend and a much better human being. I am proud to own his loyal friendship.

Next in line is **Abhishek Verma**, he is a very generous person, kind hearted, tall and thin and always wears a stylish pair of specs. He is crazy about new mobiles and Hindi songs. He is a very good poet and is best with the sad ones. When he is in a bad mood, his anger is unmatchable. He is loved by all, admired by all and his friendship gives a sense of security. He is my 3 am friend. He possess good looks and a smart personality, so polite by tongue and clean by heart, always smiling and spreading the magic of smile and his words. He brings the words to life in his poems and always lightens the mood everywhere no matter whether he is sad or happy. We've always considered his shyness as his weakness. My life smiles at me when I am in his company, love you bro!

Here comes the friend of friends, **Lavanya Banerjee**. I've given her so many names, my favourite one is 'Doraemon', and she resembles him when she is angry or when she smiles. She offers her hand when I fall, she lends her shoulder when I cry, and she hugs me when I am happy. When she is angry, she is like the cup of hot coffee, which is very difficult to handle but I am habitual of the taste of this hot coffee! Such a great friend I have, she is the most precious gem of my treasure of friendship.

**Himani Goel**, well known as Himi, is another one of my friends who keep me happy. She is crazy, but a lovely girl. She is the cutest person I've ever met, always singing around, loves gossiping and enjoys company of friends. She always understands the need of time. She listens well even if I am speaking senseless talks; she fully admires me and believes in me. She is a good scholar as well as a music lover. I've never seen her angry so can't predict what will happen when she will be angry but I guess she'll smile then also because she has not learnt to be angry.

**Sahil Rai**, he is the man behind many of my good times. He can make you laugh anytime by sharing adult jokes and talks. He is best described by his well-built physique, sexy hair style, tall body, cute smile, sparkling eyes, and a proper dressing sense. He is a lover of fashion and is always updated. I call him the 'Sexy Beast'. His knowledge of geography is appreciable. He is a good hearted guy who is a flirt and sometimes a sincere lover also. Sometimes he is so funny that his company can make you forget the time passing by. He is the man of resources, a true gem of friendship! He is fearless, independent and always taking up the challenges. *Gaaliyan to bus zubaan pe rehti hai.* If he is there then I am sure to enjoy my life in any of the situations, he inspires me to be happy, to live the life and to be who you are. Hats off to him!!!

I called up Kshitij and said, 'Bro …plan out something yaar…getting bored at home man….'

He replied, 'I was just about to call you. We are meeting at Donald's Bakery in an hour; I've already told everyone, and you better be there on time'.

Donald's is a confectionery shop in Kidwai Nagar area where our esteemed institute, 'Mercy Memorial School' is. That shop is actually a hub of students of various schools, nearby. Daily around 2 pm, there can be seen a mob of students in different uniforms. Students of different age groups can be seen there and like every other group we assumed our gang to be the coolest one.

Okay!! I reached the Donald's as per Kshitij's order and was not on time as always. It is 4:30 in the evening. I came riding on my bicycle all the way from my home. Kshitij and Abhishek were already waiting when I joined them. As always, I was greeted with a BANG!!! '*Haramkho*r, don't you have a watch? Is this the time to come? Do you even care for how long we both are waiting for you…idiot', yelled Abhishek.

I replied very gently, 'Oye!! Don't shout bro…. sorry for getting late' and smiled at him.

Now we were waiting for the girls to come, after 15 minutes we could see an image of a girl, approaching us and by her way of walking I could tell that she was Lavanya, a big bag on her right shoulder and hair properly clipped, anyone among the three of us can identify her, we were so much familiar with her walking. Finally after half an hour, everyone had assembled.

'Okay! Let us order something to eat…so tell me who wants to eat what?' I asked everyone and I knew the answer.

Himani replied, 'Hey Kavya, did you come to eat or to meet? Wait for some time and then we'll eat… is it necessary that we should eat as soon as we arrive?'

Abhi said, 'One Paneer patty for me and one cheese burger for *budhau*'

Kshitij was called budhau because of his way of walking.

No other girl ordered anything. Then finally I ordered patties, burger and ice-cream for everyone. I and Kshitij were surprised to see that when we had finished our snacks, those girls were still on with those small patties. I wondered if they were really sophisticated or just pretending.

'I am 100% sure bro that at home they all eat like they will not get it again and look at them here, real actors they are- such hypocrites', whispered Kshitij in my ear. I had to bite my tongue to control the laughter.

All of a sudden the whole topic was changed to the boards' results which were to be announced anytime in the month of May. Every one of us knew he or she would get good marks so there was no fear in our minds. Then the debate had a new topic and that was about one of our classmates. She was cute but a bit plump. She was teased with the name of '*Chhota Haathi*', and the name had gained a good popularity. Actually our dear friend Abhi had a crush on her. Kshitij was trying to make him realize the truth, he said, 'Bro from which angle does she look good to you?'

I corrected Kshitij and said, 'Whaatt!!! Angle? My genius brother Kshitij, where did you find an angle in her? *Har jagah se to gol hai wo...* ' and believe me that was a true moment of great laughter, even the public nearby who could overhear our talks couldn't stopped laughing.

Poor Abhi, we just broke his heart, sorry for that bro!! And to the girl- we didn't intend any offence.

'Okay! Now it is getting late…we should leave now…we will meet tomorrow!' said our studious star, Lavanya.

I can bet that that was the first sentence I heard from her in those hours.

'Meeting is postponed to tomorrow' came a swift reply from Abhi. 'Bye', said Himi and then it was raining 'BYEs'.

'I am also present yaar' I said in a funny tone to Lavanya and Himi.

'Of course! Bye Kavya', replied both of them.

We exchanged smiles and after 15 minutes the girls left. We lingered a while longer to plan something for next morning but unfortunately nothing could be decided.

# Chapter Four

It was the eve of 17ᵗʰ May, 2010 and we all were once again at Donald's point This time I was the first one to arrive but within no time Kshitij and Abhishek came, and like always Sahil didn't show up. Girls were late again. They kept us waiting for 40 minutes, such VIPs they are! First Himi came and then came Lavanya. It was all going so well when out of nowhere, a sound came, 'Hi everyone!!' for one second I felt like killing him but when he spoke the second sentence, 'Hey Girls, How are you all?', then that very moment I was searching for a knife, either to stab him or to put it inside myself. Only god knew how much I hated him.

Okay! He is **Harsh Chaudhary**; I guess every other guy hated him or I can say was envious of him because of his popularity with the girls. May be I was jealous too. One thing was sure he was not invited there but the truth was he was standing right in front of us. Anyways, we all avoided him except girls, girls were very fond of him and even today they are. He was the dude, he had the guts to talk and the skills, he had a great sense of humour, and he was notorious and always had a correct timing!

His arrival was not welcomed by us. But what to do, now he was there and as per our expectations, he started, 'Lavanya, you are looking very beautiful today, a bit different...'

*Oh wow! What a pickup line it was!!!*

I don't know why but I always wanted to hit this monkey whenever he spoke this kind of sentences.

'Different? What different? I always look like this only' replied Lavanya half smiling and a bit blushing.

Oh god! I just can't understand what was the need to take this conversation to the next level? She could have easily appreciated his complement and stopped the further discussions on her looks but no! *Girls are girls!!*

'No, not always but today is something different, *what is the matter?'* he asked in a mischievous way and we all knew her reply and that was, 'Shut up!!!'

Then we heard words from Himi and I just wanted to go and lay down on the adjoining road. 'You too are looking different! Found a girl or what?? Or Lavanya accepted your proposal?' Himi encouraged that moron to talk further.

Abhi, Kshitij and I exchanged bored glances.

'Shut up Himi' Lavanya intervened.

'Arey no no, I am not that lucky yaar', Chaudhary expressed his ultimate sorrow.

'Ha ha ha ha ha! Very funny' was the obvious reply from Lavanya.

It seemed that these national matters of her different looks would not end soon and then the much awaited sentence, *'Saale! Haramkhor*! Just shut up else I'll make you feel unlucky right now... who invited you?' Abhi shouted and his frustration and anger was clearly visible.

Chaudhary could not believe his ears; he was under shock for at least 15 seconds but then gathered his senses and in a very soft frightened tone he said, 'Arey What happened bro? Why are you getting furious?' and started laughing as if Abhi had cracked an award winning joke. It was just to hide his humiliation.

My full sympathies were with him and when everything came back to normal again, Abhi dropped another bomb of his anger, 'Now if you speak out any more nonsense, I'll break your jaws, I swear.'

I can't tell you how much pleasure Kshitij and I was having all this time.

'Now stop it yaar Abhishek' said Himi, trying to cool down the situation

Lavanya also said, '*Ha yaar bus karo*, now he is not saying anything then also you are over reacting Abhi' and then turning towards me and Kshitij, she said, 'Will you both say something or just keep on standing like statues, why don't both of you stop Abhi?'

We both just nodded our heads and said, 'Hmmm Hmmm'.

Half an hour passed before we got anything to eat. The main purpose of gathering there was to discuss the next day's plan as the next day our results were to be announced. We were all ready for the results. 'What is the plan for tomorrow?' I asked excitedly.

'What plan? We will check the result, what else?' replied Himi.

'And what after the results, *dhakkans!*' I asked again, irritated.

'That we will see…first let the results come…if any plan is made, then everyone will be informed….' Lavanya suggested.

I kept quiet because I knew any further discussions with them will turn out to be an argument. It is truly said that any discussion with a woman is an argument and no man on this earth can win any kind of argument with a woman. I was thinking this and was smiling unknowingly.

'Why are you smiling? Did I crack a joke??' asked Lavanya as she noticed me

'Nothing! Okay! Let's go and all the best for tomorrow' I said. We went home, our minds occupied with next day's anticipation.

The next morning was bright and sunny. I knew that results might be out anytime. There was some uneasiness in my stomach and I was noticing every detail of the day, trying to figure out whether it was a good day or bad. I read the newspaper and came to know that class tenth results will be announced at around 2 pm. No matter how confident I was, my mind started getting clouded with doubts, trying to recall if my exams had gone really good or not. I informed Kshitij, Abhishek and Sahil to be at my place before 2 pm. That helped but little. I didn't eat much that day; my appetite had substantially shrunk that day to just a slice of bread and half a glass of milk. Somehow I managed to spend the time till 2 pm and then they all arrived on their bicycles. After a long try we could access the official site of ICSE. Now the tension was at its peak.

The question of the moment was *kiska result sabse pehle dekha jaaye?* Exactly at that time our brave-heart Abhi entered his roll number and we all stared at the screen, waiting for the result to load. Slowly the result page opened from top to bottom. When we were just about to see the full page, the internet connection was lost all of a sudden.

'*Iski maa ki.....*' shouted Abhishek.

'Even God is joking with you Abhishek' remarked Kshitij and laughed a lot, then remembering that we were in my home I shouted, 'Hey....talk softly...and don't abuse... we are at home. Okay, let us go to the cyber cafe!!'

We could just see his English marks, which were not very good and it made our mind prepared for something bad. Thankfully cafe was near my home, we all rushed there. There was not much public. Again, Abhishek was the first one to look for his result. We were anxious. This time something different happened at that very stage, where we were about to see the result page, the monitor went out.

*Oh man!!*

Abhi was having a bad day, we switched over to the next system and this time he refused to see his result first so it was Sahil who showed some courage and entered his roll number, and to our surprise his result was not as expected. He was expecting at least 90% but had got only 86%. He was one of the most studious among us. We thought if he had secured only this much then we stood nowhere. 'Don't waste time in gossiping and laughing, just enter your roll number Kavya' shouted Kshitij in a tensed voice.

I obeyed him and entered the roll number and crossed my fingers. '91%', I shouted happily. I was glad.

'Now it's your turn Kshitij, tell me the roll number' I asked him, although I knew it. He gave me a terrifying look. I understood and let him continued with the process, '92.6%', he shouted and jumped in excitement and lastly it was again Abhishek's turn. His first two attempts were almost like a heart fail for him.

He entered his roll number again and waited, this time everything was right, no power cut, no loss of net connection, but this time site stopped. *Oh God! Was it some kind of mystery?*

We laughed and laughed. 'Laugh…laugh, I'll score the highest among us and then you will all cry and I will laugh' he said.

After lot of struggle, finally his result was out, '92.8%' he shouted, danced and said, 'Like I said my boys, like I said!!!'

We were in the state of total confusion whether to celebrate our results or to show sympathy to Sahil. He also scored well but as it is said that 'it hurts when a friend scores more than you'. After a deep thought we stood calm there.

'Oye, it's okay! Let us celebrate!!' said Sahil after understanding the whole scenario.

His words relaxed us. Then I called Lavanya and after two or three rings her mother picked up the phone and that was totally unexpected, I didn't know what to say now and also couldn't cut the line. After summoning a lot of courage, I said, 'Namastey Aunty! Is Lavanya there? I am Kavya' and closed my eyes.

'Namastey beta, she is checking her result, by the way what was your result?' she asked. That was the question she was not supposed to ask but I replied, 'Not very good, I've secured 91%'. She replied on the other side, 'Arey it is nice… you have secured good marks, okay! Lavanya is here'.

*'Aur madame, kitna raha?'* I asked. '93%' she replied.

'Oh! Good! Congrats, I guess, its your party in the evening?' I asked and waited for the obvious answer from her, 'Party! For what? I have secured 93% only, and this result cannot be the reason to give a treat.'

For a minute, I felt like going somewhere to die, to go and jump from height. I mean 93% seemed less to her, what did she want, 103%? I replied her, 'It is quite a good result yaar!… you are a topper. Let's meet in the evening'.

We all gathered again at the Donald's in the evening and this time I was the last one to enter the premises. I looked at my watch just to be sure that I am in time or not? I was 5 minutes before time and to my surprise they all were even before time. 'Waah! Its amazing…. every one is before time today? Is something special?' I entered expressing my surprise.

'We are Mercians, always before time' Himi answered proudly.

'Excuse me! It is always ahead of time, not before time' I corrected her.

Actually this was the tagline of 'Mercy Memorial School', one of the finest schools in Kanpur.

'Now will you both stop showing off your knowledge…. just shut up!' said Kshitij.

We spent more than 3 hours there and captured many beautiful moments in our cameras. That was one of the best evenings we had in our lives. I wish I could stop the time there and then only! With lots of chit chats, fights, arguments, food, cold-drinks and love that evening passed by. I was not aware of what life had planned next for me. That realization struck us like a lightening but we had to accept it. I never thought that these evenings, fun, carefree moments in the classroom will not be the same for me anymore!!

# Chapter Five

'So what have you decided?' asked dad. 'I don't know dad, I am not sure about it, I've not decided yet what to do in life, give me some time, I'll let you know' I replied.

'Time? How much more time do you need now? You've passed your tenth and you should have a sense of responsibility now. You should know what to do in life. Do you have any seriousness or sincerity; boys of your age very well know that what they have to do in life and you haven't even given a thought to it? *Apne bachpane se bahar aao samajh aaya*, it's time to get serious now, and show some serious attitude towards life and improve your daily routine and habits, I don't like pointing it always' like a typical father he scolded me.

'Now why are you standing like a dumb? Did you hear what I said? I want an answer till the evening…think properly….' he ordered and went to his office.

'Yaar he is not ready to understand anything, what should I do then? All day he has only this topic to talk on…he can win a debate on this topic…let me first finish my XII and then I'll decide what to do….why are you guys pressurising me?' I argued with mom now.

'Why are arguing with me? Argue with your dad, *tab bolti band rehti hai waise sher bane ghoomte firte ho,* I'll try to talk to him but you will have to talk to him in the end.' she replied.

'Love you mom!!' I shouted and was about to leave the home when suddenly I saw an admission form.

I went closer and read it and it just gave me a heart-attack for a while, I just can't believe what I saw, I was in shock that how could dad do this to me? It is completely unfair. I didn't know how to react, whether to shout or to cry or to do what? I lost my senses.

I lost my temper and I shouted angrily, 'What the hell is this now? Is this some kind of joke or what? Without even discussing with me, he decided to change my school?? Listen carefully mom, I am not leaving MMS, and that is for sure and don't force me to do that. And why shall I change it?? *Kya kharabi dikhti hai isme?* I am not going to another school, understand well both of you? And now I am going to Kshitij's home….will return in the evening…bye.'

She tried to say something, 'wait….listen…. Kavya' but I was gone.

In a very depressed mood I went to Kshitij's home but he was not at home, his mom informed me. 'Bloody idiot, *kaam ke waqt gayab rehta hai*' I murmured.

After waiting for 15 minutes he came with his monstrous dog, Sammy. He looked more handsome than Kshitij. I was very afraid of dogs and spiders and still am. I stood behind the tree and waited for him to take his dog inside, it was a Tibetan breed, massive built up, black shining bag of fur it was, red eyes, big teeth and long legs, always a wicked smile kind of thing on its face shows as if in any second I'll be running round the whole Kidwai Nagar to save my life from that beast from hell! Finally he kept his monster inside the house and came out; we both went to the park in front of his house and got ourselves seated on the benches there.

'What happened bro?? You are looking very depressed and troubled?' investigated Kshitij.

'Dad is planning to change my school, it is some CBSE school in Ratanlal Nagar. I don't know the full story behind it but I just saw the admission form of it….that's it'

'Are you mad? What are you talking about man? And why will he do that??' he shouted surprised.

'I don't know bro…I'll talk to him about this when he will return from the office in the evening…but I am 100% sure that school is changed for me now…I can guarantee it.'

'It is not going to happen…we will talk to uncle about this….you just chill…and don't worry' he comforted me with his words.

'Let's go somewhere…just lighten up your mood.' he said in a gentle way.

By that time we all had learnt how to ride bike and how to drive a car. Kshitij then took out his auto-machine, a black Ford Figo, which looked awesome, her curves were the best part of her body, I took over the driving seat and it was a fun in driving her, what a pick-up she had.

It is my habit of changing gear pattern from $1^{st}$ to $3^{rd}$ without using the $2^{nd}$ gear and I did the same here. '*Abe chutiye!* Is $2^{nd}$ gear made for show? You are just decreasing the efficiency man…..who drives like this?' Kshitij expressed his anger.

He was a great lover of cars and so he wanted everyone to respect cars, and drive them properly. *Okay man I respect your feelings!!*

We stopped at Abhi's home and called him outside by honking the horn many times. He was in his shorts and a loose fitted red t-shirt that looked super cool.

'Come and be seated…quick!' shouted Kshitij and without wasting any minute he was in the car the very next second!

'Bro….at least wear your slippers…' I said pointing to his feet.

*'Zyada chacha mat bano, gaadi chalao chup chaap'* was the very familiar and expected reply from him.

Our car started once again and stopped at Sahil's home now. He was already standing out of the house buying some vegetables from the street seller. Now that was a perfect moment of laughter. He didn't see us. He was in his black shorts and was topless as always just to show his muscular body.

'I've confusion' I said while driving.

'What confusion?' inquired Abhishek

*'Bhai ye batao ye saala Sahil kya raat me kapde pehanta hoga ya nanga so jata hai saala'* I said.

All I could hear was laughter; even the volume of songs which were playing in the car was inaudible now and I also bursted into laughter.

'I am serious yaar…just look at him yaar….He is always semi nude…., bro, I am 1000% sure that while sleeping he takes off the bottoms also….' I said again and this time Kshitij added, 'Hmmmm, quite possible but just think that if *rat me toilet jaaye to lower utaarne ka jhanjhat hi nahi'*

Now what could be funnier than that, we just can't control our laughter, I stopped the car in the middle and laughed very much, I was unstoppable so I handed the steering to Kshitij and kept laughing imagining the situation.

'Just click his photo Kavya...quick...' Abhishek said to me with full energy but somehow I couldn't get a shot and we gave Sahil a horn, he immediately went in and wore a shirt and came directly in the car.

'Offo! Feeling very shy in front of us….we are not gay…. *Ham log ko dekhte hi shirt pehan li….?*' asked Kshitij.

Before Sahil could reply anything I asked, 'Dude! Can I say something? Don't feel bad…'

'Of course buddy! Say it' he replied.

'It was quite difficult for us to find out you between you and the *sabjiwala*' I said and immediately started to laugh.

He banged me from behind and said what was totally expected, 'you son of a bitch'.

We laughed and laughed and laughed, we'd no idea where we were going, I just forgot the bad news of the morning and I was just enjoying with them.

'We have reached Swaroop Nagar… just find a nice place to eat something' ordered Abhi.

*'Ye dekho pehanne ke liye chappal hai nahin par khana logo ko 5-star ka chahiye'* Kshitij taunted in a funny way.

'Just shut up and why don't you just park the car somewhere and find a place to eat' ordered Abhishek angrily.

Finally we parked the car outside the famous Pandit Ji's Maggie point in Swaroop Nagar and Abhi came out *nangey pair.* We've walked only few steps when we discovered that the shop was closed.

Kshitij laughed and turned to Abhi and said, *'Jab kismet me likha ho l@#\*a toh kahaan se milega pakauda'.*

Wow! What a sentence it was and the funny part of it was to see Abhi and Kshitij running on the road, Abhi looked like a mad beggar of the street who was running behind Kshitij as if Kshitij had stolen a penny from his bowl. It was an enjoyable moment but the enjoyment didn't end there, Kshitij had given the keys to me after parking at Maggie point so me and Sahil rushed into the car and were lost in the streets.

They both were now in the state of terror but could easily make out that neither car nor we were present so they must be hiding somewhere. I was thinking of Abhishek, he was in shorts, without specs, loose t-shirt and bare footed, *bus koi use pagal na samajh le* and this fear made me drove back to them. Finally we were on our way back when something more funny took place;

I swear to god that I'll never sit in a car when Sahil is driving.

We were about to take a left turn from Devki chauraha, kakadeo when suddenly a tempo passed us with only a distance of few inches, Sahil applied the brakes and car stopped then and there only.

'Are you insane?' I shouted shockingly.

'it is not my fault.... if that *tempowala* was driving recklessly then what could I do? I also indicated the turn bro' Sahil defended himself.

'Just follow him…that tempo…quickly' I screamed like hell.

I don't know why I said that but I guess some adrenaline rushed through my body which gave birth to these words.

'Arey leave it yaar…why are you risking it man?? He'll smash each and every one of us here only…in the car' said Kshitij.

'uski *aisi ki taisi*' responded Abhishek angrily and turning towards Sahil he said, 'Sahil bro…you just do what Kavya says, I've full faith in his plans'

Sahil felt like he is in the formula racing championship and he is Sebastian Vetel and that tempowala is Lewis Hamilton or maybe he thought that it is a film sequence of 'Fast and Furious', I don't know what the hell he thought but my heart was in my mouth for the next 2 minutes.

'Just slow down and bring me next to this *tempowala,* I've a brilliant pill of laughter' I instructed Sahil and he followed it.

I was sitting on the passenger seat and now his ugly face was visible to me, he was eating pan masala and when he discovered that we were neither overtaking him nor letting him do that he spoke by adjusting his masala in his mouth, 'Kya *hua bhai??'*

I asked, *'Bhai ye Star mall jaane ka rastey bataana'.*

He slowed down his tempo and so did we, it appeared as if the vehicles were not moving, we were that much slow and then the moment arrived, as soon as he took his head out to give me the directions, I hit him and I hit him hard, I slapped him so hard that all his masala was on the road, thankfully he didn't spit on me and we just speeded the vehicle. For 5-10 minutes he must be in complete shock that why I slapped him as he didn't knew he just risked our lives few kilometres back.

We laughed very much, Kshitij and Abhishek on the back seat were rolling in laughter and so did I.

'Kavya, it was a solid *chamaat*.....seriously man…I'll never mess with you!!' exclaimed Abhishek.

We came back from where we've started and now Kshitij said, 'Apart from all these jokes, serious news, Kavya is changing school.'

'W-h-a-a-a-t-t-t!!' shouted Abhishek. Sahil wondered why?

'Dad brought the form…I'll talk to him in the evening and then will tell you what happened'

# Chapter Six

I waited for dad to come home and when he came, I directly asked, '*Kisse se puch ke aap ye forms laaye hain?* I am not changing the school....do you get it?'

He replied, 'Oh! I was going to tell you about this...it's good that you saw it yourself....so what have you decided?'

'Arey...what decision? Let me first finish with my class 12th, then I'll decide something...but not now....' I answered him unwillingly. He was now making me lose my temper again and I shouted, 'And people upgrade their school... not degrade it...I mean...they change for a better school and you've brought the form of a just *aiwai* school?? Am I wasting your money in this school or am I not getting good marks or have I not scored well in class tenth? What is it?'

'Don't act and talk like a mad man....have you ever seen your cousin, Viraat...he has always been sincere towards his studies....after 10th he himself searched for the IIT coaching and brought all the admission forms and just look at you.... you haven't yet decided what you have to do...', he continued his discussion with me.

Now I understood the whole scene, he wanted me to join a coaching institute for preparations of IIT entrance exam just like Viraat is doing; he is my cousin.

So, dad wanted me to prepare myself for the engineering exams just as Viraat was doing and for that he want me to change school and take admission in a *aiwayi* school where attendance doesn't matter and I can concentrate on coaching. *This was his master plan.*

I wondered *what is the problem with the parents of this country? No one is haapy with their children, have you seen his son? He is in a top MNC, he is an IAS officer, he has cracked IIT, and his package is this much. Arey to hell with them yaar, I mean who cares? Will they share their salary with me, and what do I have to do with them? I even don't know them but its hard to make them understand this point…for them as if IIT is the only thing to achieve in this life and like anyone who'll meet you will if ever comes to know that you were not able to crack IIT or you are not an IItian will say, 'Ab to tum baat karne layak bhi nahi ho coz you are not an IITian'*

*These people don't see anything beyond IITs and NIT.*

*So if this is the case then I can also say that, have you seen his dad? He's GM in that company, he is a scale 5 officer in a bank, he is a director in a college, but I am not supposed to say that because I am not a dad, still a son.*

*So it means the same like,* **'tumhaara khoon khoon hai, hamara khoon pani?'**

*Actually problem is of this system which considers IITian to be a GOD!! I agree it is not less than a heaven but every student has his own stamina, his own dreams,his own capability,* **saala sabke sab bus bheed me ghusne me lage hai, akele chalne me sab darte hai.** *The fear of what people will think if their children are not an IITian is spoiling the country's future.*

'**What people will think**' *has killed more dreams than anything else in this country....No one ever thinks that what his child would think....it is of least concern to them. Sorry to say but the public of this country is not ready to accept the truth...no matter how much any one explains them but they are not ready to understand.*

*Everyone liked '***Taare Zameen Par***' aur '**3 Idiots**',but did these movies not give the same message? In reality no one ever learnt anything from such great movies. India is the country for maximum suicides and among them maximum are the cases of depression and from where this depression take birth? The answer is very clear, this society, fear of society gave birth to this depression. Parents force their children to join engineering or medicine and result proves to be very fatal. Even after this much, they don't understand, for them their respect, their image is much more valuable than their children! I just wish I could get out from this system!*

*(I am not thinking this because I was forced to do engineering; I've always wanted to be in an engineering college but not like this, by sacrificing my school days. I could study in any engineering college and could get a placement, I'll get some salary to survive quite fine but this is not acceptable to my dad. IIT is the call and if not IIT then not less than NIT.)*

'Arey! Why do you not understand? I have no interest in doing any kind of coachings and if I will do it then it is for sure that I'll do it after 12th but why now? *Engineering hi toh karni hai*, is it a compulsion to do it from IIT?? And as far as packagae is considered, then there is no need to waste time on it, now.....? I'll adjust even if I'll get placed with less package.... the degree of BE will not get wasted..... and why are you comparing it with Viraat? What the hell have I got to do with him?? Just stop this comparing habit of yours.... just try to understand that there is no need to take coachings at this stage and there are many engineers who are not IITians yet they are earning more than the IITians....not everyone get placed even in IITs....and this is the topic to discuss later but for now if I change my school, I'll miss my fun and friends...will I ever get these days back? To be successful doesn't mean to leave everything dad and motto of life is not only to earn money but also to enjoy these moments which you can cherish. Just remember that money can't buy happiness but these memories certainly can. Listen dad, neither am I changing school nor am I joining any coaching institute' I said in a frustrating and in a fully filmy tone.

It seemed like a scene of a Hindi movie was in progress where a father and son had a clash.

'First of all don't forget that you are talking to your dad so show some respect and secondly stop using these filmy dialogues. Be practical and now let me give you the reason to join coachings now, first reason is that by joining now you will have two attempts to appear in the competition exams so it automatically increases your chances of getting selected in a better institute and the second reason is that if in the first attempt you cannot make it to an IIT then in the second attempt you can try....and now you have to take a stand for your studies, life and future.... Now is your age to think beyond masti, to take your career seriously, don't ruin your life beta', he tried to make me understand.

'Arey just look at yourself only. Till today you are only earning money. Which was the last movie you watched with your family or friends? When was the las time you took us for an outing? You work from morning to evening, people respect you, we love you but can you say that you love yourself? Are you happy with your life? With the way you've spent your last 25 years in just collecting cash? Okay, let me ask you when was the last time you drove the car above 100? What is that thing from your past that you could remember and smile? You can't? Coz for that one needs to have memories but I am sorry to say that I don't want a life like you.... I want to smile, want to laugh in future.' I changed the whole scene now, discussion took another form, now the matter of concern was not IIT or coaching but it was now something else, something I should not have said, after all he was my father, how could I blame him like this? He had sacrificed many of his meetings for me.

I felt guilty but *the words were already out.*

My eyes were wet and my volume increased in my previous sentences. I was so sorry.

'Please stop thinking for me... I've spent my life very well so far and will continue to do the same in future and I remember everything, my school friends are with me even today and as far as the car is considered, still today I drive it at a speed of 100 and you know it well, so you got your answers? So just stop irritating me with your idiotic views, I am very happy and if you still have the same philosophy then you'll not laugh in future but your future will laugh at you. I am not angry, nor disappointed in you, it was the most expected reply from you as always, you are so filmy, now let's come back to the topic, if you don't then want we'll not force you further, he said and somewhere his disappointment was visible.

Although I was still angry and frustrated, somewhere down there he had me convinced.

'Okay I am ready and I am sorry for the way I talked and behaved, I am sorry' and hugged him. I agreed and thought *jo hota hai, achche ke liye hota hai* and I had just turned to my room when he stopped me, 'Kavya one more thing'

'Yes, say it dad'

'You asked me, what is that thing from the past that I can remember and smile even today?'

'Yes. I asked....so?'

'So the answer is that it was the date 2nd August-1994, this is something from the past which brings a smile on face. When you and Kanika were the only reason for my smile'

My eyes welled with tears.

'Oh.... Dad... I am sorry'

*(It was the birth date of me and my twin sis Kanika- I'll introduce her later)*

I hugged him and went inside my room. Some voice inside me was still arguing, '*if any one who can secure 90 plus in his tenth then according to his parents, he is made to be an IItian... what a crap!!*' But that voice very small and it didn't matter now. I pushed it aside and drifted to sleep.

Next morning I narrated the whole conversation to Kshitij and Sahil when I met them.

After thinking deeply Kshitij said, 'Yaar its okay, what can you do now? Just do as your dad says...he is thinking correctly and you also know that in this school coachings are not possible...and we all will be meeting daily bro.... we have more fun outside than in the classroom so you won't miss anything'

I understood what he was trying to say and when Sahil echoed him, I agreed on changing the school.

Next person whom I wanted to meet was Lavanya; I called her and asked her to meet me. I asked, 'Can we meet at star mall in the evening?? I've something to talk about. And bring Himi along if you can'

'Okay' she said a little unsure.

So we agreed to meet at star mall at 5 in the evening

It was 5 pm and I was waiting in the food court for both of them and then they came. 'What is the matter? Inquired Lavanya.

'Arey wait wait...have some patience my girl, first let us order something' I replied.

After eating the delicious Domino's pizza I started, 'Actually yaar I am changing school, so I thought of meeting everyone'

'Wh-a-a-a-a...a-a-a-t!!!!' both the girls cried out loud.

'But Why??' asked Lavanya and then I narrated the whole drama to both of them.

'Oh! So this is the matter...it is quite serious...in fact I also have to join this coaching but I'll join after class 12 coz I can't afford to change my school but it doesn't mean that you should also not change it....' responded Himi.

'Now what can you do...in fact what can anyone of us do? We all have to separate someday after 12$^{th}$ but don't take tension Kavya, I am always with you in every situation and never feel yourself to be sad or alone, I am with you, you just concentrate on the purpose for which you've to change the school, I am with you like your shadow' these words from Lavanya made my day, there was so much care hidden in them.

'And so do I' said Himi.

A tear rolled down my cheek before I could hold back, and I immediately wiped it.

'H-a-a-w-w-w! Don't cry, we'll always be together, we can't fight with our fate, and stop crying now dear' said Lavanya.

After hearing this, number of tears gradually increased but I controlled the situation.

'Yaar Kavya I've never seen you crying... I never thought that you could be so emotional' Himi expressed her surprise and wiped her wet eyes. Within no time Lavanya also took out her hanky and start wiping her eyes. It is always this contagious with ladies.

'Enough of it now, lets go before we flood this area', I tried to lighten the mood and we all came out of the mall, talked for a while and then parted.

I went home and told everyone that I was ready to take admission in whatever school they wished. Dad took out the form for me to fill it up and I did accordingly.

'Okay then tomorrow go and bring the forms of your coaching also' he said.

'But I don't want to go so far to bring the forms... please while returning from the office, you only bring them na?' I expressed my objection.

'You just kill the time whole day... just go and bring the forms of coaching of Sandeep Chauhan, Ajay Vishwaas and Naman Tyagi.... *mere ghar aane se pehle forms aa jaye....*' his voice was stern this time.

These three were the best teachers in whole Kanpur. Chemistry by Sandeep Chauhan, Mathematics by Ajay Vishwaas and Physics by Naman Tyagi!

'Okay, I will go', I had no other choice and then switched on the T.V.

# Chapter Seven

I woke up next morning. I was in half sitting and half lying position and my eyes were half open and half closed. I wanted to sleep again but now it was all laziness only. For five-to ten-minutes I thought something about the previous day and the decision I took, I wondered if I had taken a wrong decision but then stopped thinking further. I looked the watch, it was only 9 O'clock and I slept again for five minutes but when I opened my eyes again, it was 11 O'clock.

Suddenly I was so active because I remembered that I'd to bring the forms before 6 pm. I just jumped out of bed and landed directly into the bathroom, took a shower and went downstairs. Obviously it was not the time for breakfast and all the food from the dining table had been kept back into the kitchen.

'Mom' I shouted but she didn't answer. 'Mom' I shouted again, this time louder but again no reply came.

I called her then, 'Hello, Where are you?'

I am in the market with your dad... you were sleeping so I didn't disturb... what happened?' she asked.

'No... Nothing happened...I just called to tell that I am leaving to bring the forms...'

'Did you have your breakfast?? Don't dare to leave home without eating'

'Yes, I had my breakfast and now bye'.

I locked the home and kicked the bike, a Hero Honda Passion, and left the home. I had hardly covered a kilometre when I saw Abhi and Sahil going towards my house on their scooters.

I shouted, 'Sahil, Abhishek, here.....where are you going?'

'Turn turn turn' shouted Sahil and they both stopped beside me.

'Where are you going?' asked Abhi.

'Kakadeo, to bring the forms... if you both want you can join me, what say?' I asked.

'Yes, why not? Let's go' replied Sahil.

We again started our vehicles and were off to kakadeo and of course it changed into a race where no one came first. Soon we reached our destination. We parked our vehicles in front of the huge building of the very famous Sandeep Chauhan.

'Chemistry for IIT-JEE by- Sandeep Chauhan, Inderjeet Singh and Alok Chauhan', it was the only thing written on the big board above the gate. The building was well crafted and decorated with dark blue glass. It looked nothing less than a mall. It was beautifully built and had an underground parking for the students. It was still under construction. We entered the building and straight away went in the reception area. It was a huge room whose two adjacent walls were decorated with a very nice texture and the other two were not walls but were transparent glasses. The big desk of the receptionist was also no less fascinating, but the minus point was the receptionist. The biggest drawback was that the receptionist was a man.

*A total disappointment!*

He was tall, he had dirty hair which were not been washed from the day he was born, and when he smiled, he looked more dangerous as his black teeth were visible; it clearly showed how much he loved *pan masaala*. There were two sofas for the public to sit and enjoy the cool atmosphere and see the TV which was adjusted somehow on the wall. After taking a good look on the whole building, its office, reception and parking lot, we went to look around for water and the security guard led us there.

Actually the purpose was just to look around the place, to explore it. The whole place was quite well finished and nice. I liked it. We took the form and left. Our next stop was Physics institute which was 2-3 blocks away from the chemistry institute. We entered the building, the most stylish building of the whole kakadeo. The reception area was also very nice, but the same problem, receptionist was again a man. We took the form and stopped next at Vishwaas Classes, the perfect institute of maths and the best instructors- Ajay Vishwaas & Ankur Vishwaas. Here also we collected the form with the same disappointment and went back home.

'Kakadeo is exactly the same as I've heard of' Abhishek said.

'Hmmm' I replied.

'It seemed that many students come here...parking was more than full' Sahil said.

'So?? It is obvious...have you never heard of kakadeo?? There are minimum 500-600 students in a single batch. Have you never heard of it? Seriously? Then you are a real villager? hehehehehe' laughed Kshitij.

And then came the very much expected reply from Sahil, 'Why don't you just shut the fuck up? You are saying as if you are the owner of this coaching hub?' At last I had to interfere 'Alright alright...just stop it man... it's nothing to discuss about', I said. 'Okay... so Kavya when are the new batches commencing from?? I mean how much time do you have?' asked Abhi.

We all looked each other in surprise and then together we shouted in an astonished manner, 'How much time do you have?? What does that even mean?'

'Bro... I guess from 2nd of June' I replied.

'Oh!! Good... so you are left with hardly 10-12 days of enjoyment...okay then let us celebrate and party hard' Abhi replied.

'Yes, said exactly the right thing buddy...we all will remain in the school but our Kavya bro will not be there with us so for Kavya, let us make him feel special' added Sahil.

'Hmmm..... after few days he will get busy in his new life, coaching and all...so from tomorrow only....let's party boys' said Kshitij and laughed in a mischievous way or like it was a devil's laugh!!

'Arey! It's okay..... I am not dying bro... Thanks.....okay and if you guys plan out something cool then let me know' I replied.

Then again in the evening we gathered at Sahil's, but here we got into trouble, we never expected that though.

It was around 5:30 pm and we all were sitting in the drawing room. I was late as always and was welcomed with the *Gaaliyan* of Sahil, '*Kutte!* You wear a *ghanta,* not a watch and then also you are always late.... you are a black spot on the name of Mercians'.

(*Actually the tag line of Mercy Memorial School was 'ALWAYS AHEAD OF TIME'*)

I defended myself by saying, 'Bro... Relax...calm down.... sorry yaar...actually the bike was punctured'

'And why are you wearing this watch in your right hand like girls...are you a girl?' asked Kshitij.

I smiled and avoided the further discussion.

'So my dear brothers....today I've something very special for you all... after watching this *tum sab mere ehsaan ke neechey dab jaoge*' said Sahil. I wondered why the hell did he used that *ehsaan ke neeche dab jaane wali* line, I mean could he not find any worse line than that?

Anyways, he stood up and went inside. After few minutes he returned with the most horrible thing, our maths book, 'ISC CONSICE MATHEMATICS'.

'Have you gone mad??' shouted Abhi.

'Yes..... Are you in your senses?? You want to study maths now and this is something special as you said?' asked Kshitij.

Then Sahil cleared all the confusion, 'Wait for a second... you impatient idiots...Abhi...open page number 147 and take out that memory card'.

'Okay!!' said Abhishek and he took out the memory card.

I don't know why but I kinda knew that what he had to show. I guessed it in my mind and was 100% correct when he played that shitty memory card. That memory card was loaded with *porn* movies. Actually we had a new new craze of watching it, so it was like a jackpot. Everyone watched it quietly and attentively so that not even the single scene can be missed, and the best part was the sound. Firstly, I hesitated a bit then the very next second, I was among the audience, enjoying the show. I'd to leave due to some reasons but the show was in progress. Now you might be wondering that what the trouble in it was. Have patience my friends. Trouble actually was narrated to me after few days, since I left early.

I met all of them after 3-4 days at Kshitij's home and asked, 'So Sahil buddy....where did you spent your night that day?? In the bed or in the bathroom?

*If you understand what I mean!*

'Don't ask dude..... *bahot bada kalesh ho gaya*..... You left early so you wee safe' he replied in a sad tone.

Then avoiding his sadness I asked, 'Okay... but tell me where you got that memory card?'

'You bitch!! I am telling you that we are totally fucked up and you are still concerned about that memory card' he shouted angrily.

I laughed and over reacted, 'Okay.... now elaborate please.... Who fucked you all?? You just take the name and we will make his life worse than hell...you just take the name....'

'*Mere baap ne bh\*$@&# kay*' he again shouted.

'Oh!! Then it is okay... but seriously man...just tell me the whole story with behind the scenes also...hehehehehe' I laughed.

Then he narrated the whole incident, 'Yaar when you left... you idiot...you kept the gate open....it all happened coz of you.....and we were in our own world-*fantasy world* and we were listening above the audible level.... and then papa entered and he watched everything...in fact heard every voice and you remained safe.....but we all got fucked up'.

I couldn't stop laughing for some time, of course it was a matter to laugh, what else was I supposed to do? I imagined the situation of uncle watching porn or at least listening to those F***ing sounds with them and I just bursted out into more laughter and I am pretty sure that Sahil would have been at his peak when uncle had arrived. Poor Sahil!! I felt sorry for him and for the others.

After sometime I replied, 'You only were getting despo.... *bahot sex ka bhoot chada tha...* now you people will think 1000 times before even doing something in your dreams.... hahahahaha.... so you guys enjoyed or not? And who the hell asked you to make it audible in whole of the neighbourhood? I was fortunate enough to leave at the right time else I also would have got fucked up with you....Go brother go... go home and spent rest of your life in embarrassment... but tell me one thing how are you facing your dad since then?'

'Don't make fun now, shit happens. And it is okay.... he'll forget it in few days but from now I just wake up after he goes to the office and sleeps before he returns....' he replied.

He added, 'Kavya, you and Abhi were the two people in the room who were super excited about it... who said that we'll watch from the first smooch till the last 'A-A-A-A-A-H-H-H-H-H-H!!!!' and who was making all that funny sounds O-O-H-H-H!! A-A-A-A-A-H-H-H-H-H!!!! A-A-A-A-A-H-H-H-H-H-H!!!! Y-E-E-E-A-A-A-H-H-H-H!!!! N-N-O-O-O-O-O!!!!   M-O-O-O-R-R-R-R-E-E-E-E!!!!! Y-E-E-A-A-A-H-H-H B-A-B-Y!!!!! H-A-A-A-A-R-R-R-R-D-D-D-D-D-E-E-R-R!!! You are just safe dude....'

Without wasting any second, I changed the topic, 'Arey!!! Leave it now yaar, ab *lanka lag hi gayi hai*, just tell me who will come for a movie tomorrow?'

Kshitij replied, 'Listen now.... Sahil's father called in our home but he just didn't tell about what happened... he just proved the saying...*live off the edge!!!* And now you go and watch the movie with your beloved Lavanya.... *Bhakk!!!*'

*Days passed away, time flew, and suddenly I realised that my best of the best friends were to depart from my life now. The life had taken a new turn, and I prayed it to be a smooth one. Past days were the old chapters and Kshitij, Abhi, Sahil, Himi, Lavanya all were just the old characters of my story. I felt sorry for myself; I didn't want to move on, my heart cried, and somewhere a fear was hidden, fear of losing them forever or the fear of being forgotten. But I had to move on with tears, I had to finish what I had started, I had to stand and stand still. By every passing second my heartbeat increased, shivering started, I was getting cold, and fear was eating me gradually and gradually. I wanted to sleep peacefully and relax but as soon as I closed my eyes flashback started in a slow motion. They were standing and calling me back but I was not able to move myself, they were disappearing, I was screaming,' I've to go to them, I've to go to them, please let me go, let go off me' and suddenly total black, complete darkness, fear was at its peak and finally I was separated and lost. I realised that my fun packed days are over and now from the next day I've to join a new world, a new chase and a new beginning. This chapter was over. Nothing will be the same from now, at least for me.*

# Chapter Eight

2<sup>nd</sup>June, 2010:

$I$t was the first day of my coaching and I had to join the classes from 2pm so me and my twin sister Kanika, who had also joined the coaching with me, were dropped to the building of Mr. Sandeep Chauhan. We had our I-cards, a notebook and a pen. We entered the building, there was a huge crowd of students and was a separate line for boys and girls to enter the classroom. We were new and so was every other student around there, no one had any idea about anything. We just did what we were instructed by the guards. They checked the I-card and allowed us to enter. The classroom was very spacious and large, we entered and grabbed a seat, and actually there were benches and tables. Within no time the hall was full of students and there was hardly any space to breathe, I guess around 400-500 students were sitting in the hall. After some time AC was turned on and we were given some sheets about the introductory chapter, 'VOLUMETRIC ANALYSIS'.

Since it was the first class, it was of short duration. Then, the genius, Mr. Sandeep Chauhan entered the hall and stepped over the platform made for the teaching purpose. He looked like one of the gatekeepers; he was more than half bald, black complexion, funny looking face with the front two teeth out of his mouth and had a very very funny style of walking, his tummy was almost touching his thighs and the first sentence he spoke was, '*Chalo beta aaj ham padhenge volumetric ananlysis, kya koi mujhe batayega ki volume kya hota hai?*'

The funny part was his accent- he pronounced volume as *valuum.*

I wondered that he is such a maestro of chemistry and accent is just worse than his gatekeeper. Anyways the class was dismissed after 13:30 hrs. After the dismissal, the whole crowd ran like mad people to get the first seats in the next class of physics; the physics institute was nearby so everyone ran including me but since I'd joined the coaching for physics in the less crowded building so I did not run so fast. I was amazed to see the view of kakadeo and entered the building. It was a very stylish coaching centre and was of just 100-150 students. We waited for the physics instructor, Mr. Naman Tyagi and finally he came. He looked like a girl, no hair on hands, no facial hair, stylish look, bouncy hair and a big smile and a very very friendly attitude towards the students.

Soon this class also got over and I and Kanika were waiting for dad to pick us when he called and said, 'I've arranged a van for you both...I've talked to its driver...he must be waiting somewhere there only...number of van is UP 78 K 5007, and the name of the driver is Naveen. I've texted his mobile number to you... call him'

Kakadeo was famous for many things like, J.K. Temple, Rave@Moti Mall, Momos, coaching of course and the very common vans. Vans used to pick up the students from their homes and drop them to the coaching and in the evening drop them back to their homes. It was a very safe mode of transport for those students who had no personal convence like bike, scooty, etc.

My van mates were of area called 'BARRA'. I called the driver and told the driver about our location so he came with his van in front of the coaching. We identified the van; it was a white color Omni van with curtains on the window. We entered the van and there were already three people sitting, 2 boys and one girl. We exchanged smiles and settled. Since we all were new here, we hesitated to talk, but then I broke the silence by saying, ' Hi! I am Kavya and she is my sister Kanika'. I got a quick reply from the first boy, 'Hi! I am Gautam'. 'Hi! I am Ambar' was the swift reply from the second boy' and 'I am Simmi' replied the girl. They seemed friendly to me.

Ambar was a tall boy of well built physique. His height was around 6'2" or 6'3", had a cute face with extra cute smile and had a big *chashma*. Gautam was also a tall fellow but not as tall as Ambar, he was thin and lean and a very shrill voice just like of a girl. Simmi was cute girl, beautiful and looked surprised, she also wore *chashma* like me and Ambar. She looked quite pretty in her floral print top and dark blue jeans. After the introduction, we took our conversation to the next level and then soon our home came, our home was the first stop of the van.

Mummy asked, 'So how was the day? Made new friends?? In van or in coachings?? And what about studies?' These words gave a sense of relief, after all mom is a mom.

'Yes mom.... it was a nice day...teachers were also cool... and understood the first topic and I guess I'll make some new friends in van...they are good people' I replied. Kanika too had similar experience.

'Good..... Okay now wash your hands and eat your dinner and if want to study then study else go to sleep...' she said.

The whole night I kept thinking about the day, it was not as bad as I'd imagined, coachings were cool, instructors were friendly, new people and van-mates were nice, nothing was wrong. I thought it as a beautiful beginning of the new chapter and slept. Never before I've waited for the next morning so eagerly, I wanted to go to the coaching so I slept.

Next morning I woke up earlier than Kanika. I felt so fresh and since school were not opened yet so I just relaxed as I knew that it was going to be very hectic when school re-opens as schools and coachings cannot run parallel to each other. Moreover, just after getting home from school I'll have to go to coaching and return late at night. But fortunately schools were still closed during the summer vacations.

Soon the clock showed 3 pm, that was the time for the van to come, driver uncle blew the horn in his style, it was like 2 times *po po* with a pause and then 3 times *po po po* without a pause and used to repeat this pattern for at least 3 times. The sound was audible from the main road. Finally the van stopped in front of my gate and as always I was again late. I wonder why I am always late.

*Late when I've to meet friends, late for everything and now late for the van!!*

I thought everyone in the van will shout at me but since we still didn't have that much tuning, no one expressed their anger. Finally I put my shoes on and opened the gate; Kanika had already gone 10 minutes before me. I was kind of 10-to-12 minutes late.

Anyways I opened the gate and saw the van but that all the curtains were down, I thought it was may be of extreme hot climate. Loo was blowing and the curtain of the window seat of the opposite seat displaced a little and all I could see was a new face. I thought may be new students have taken admission to the coaching and have joined this van and then I finally seated myself in the van. After 5 minutes I noticed the new faces, 2 boys.

One boy was sitting next to the driver's seat, his name was Yogendra, or better as Yudy. He was a small guy but with a good physique. The 2$^{nd}$ new boy was Arjun; he was fat boy, tall and strongly built.

# Chapter Nine

Then my eyes visited a perfect piece of beauty. A masterpiece created with calmness and patience. I thought how could one be so beautiful? Was she real or was I day dreaming? For the next 5-10 minutes I kept staring at her. I was in the new world. A world where only beauty existed, such shyness, such cuteness and her smile was beyond explanation. She wore a black top in an offbeat way and the multi-coloured strip pattern on it was printed very calmly and perfectly as if the manufacturer knew already that someone so beautiful was going to wear it. It was just fabulous!!! She looked irresistibly beautiful that day, the day I saw her for the very first time....

She was the perfect example of nymphs in the heaven. She looked amazingly sexy and perfectly cute at the same time. Her lips appeared to be lilac soft. Her unpinned hair was adding to her beauty. It flowed in waves to adorn her glowing, porcelain-like skin. Her eyes, framed by long velvety lashes, were a bright pair of blissful blue eyes. They were so crafted that every second when someone looks at them, he keeps on looking them. They appeared to shine like blue opalescent flowers in the lake of the palace of the heavenly angels! What to say about her smile, had she smiled, the world would sigh with contentment. Had she laughed, the world would laugh with her. And had she wept, the whole world would want to comfort her. She was irresistible. To be honest, I just fell in love with her, the very moment I saw her. Till then I didn't believed in the love at first sight but this was actually the love at first sight.

I guess something went wrong or she got uncomfortable due to my continuous staring but I was not staring, I just got lost in my thoughts but my eyes were looking her. Ambar pinched me with a wicked smile on his face.

'Oh! Sorry!' I said.

'It's okay! By the way I am Mishti' she replied.

'I am Kavya' I replied and smiled.

She smiled and turned her face to the window and I swear from the side view she looked even prettier but this time I controlled and just started talking to Ambar but my mind was thinking of her only.

I thought, 'She is so beautiful.... looking like a fairy'.

I couldn't believe that I was in love. I was so confused.

I thought, 'Attraction? Okay I'll wait for few days and then decide but this feeling ain't going away!'

Soon the van stopped in front of the Maths coaching. I was still in the thoughts when Ambar asked, 'Something happened? I know bro' and started singing-cum-teasing - *Pehli nazar me aisa jaadu kar diya, tera ban baitha mera jiya......*

I laughed, nodded my head and said, 'Shut up and move, there is nothing like what you are thinking'. I was not able to divert my mind, now everything seemed beautiful, even that ugly monstrous gate keeper looked beautiful.

I thought, 'I've said that there is nothing but is it true?' I kept thinking and thinking of her, I was lost and that was clearly visible. Somehow I entered the class room and this class room was even bigger than that of chemistry and physics one. I got myself seated from where I could see her. Then the whole place became crowded and she was lost in the crowd. I was disappointed.

Anyways, then entered the real master, the real mathematician, the very famous Mr. Ajay Vishwaas. I was in complete shock for few minutes and thought, 'oh man!! What is so special about today? I've just met two amazingly different persons...one is so beautiful - Mishti and when is so tall - Ajay Vishwaas...... he must be at least 6'4".'

Yes he was so tall and had a very dashing personality, it seemed that he never combed his hair; he had a cute smile and wore very stylish specs. He was formally dressed and looked friendly. Finally there was silence in the class but my eyes were still searching her and they found her. She was sitting very far in the first or second seat. Since I was seated on the last bench of the class, I was not able to see her properly but somehow I adjusted with the not so clear view of her. After watching her for 20-25 minutes, I looked around and then I realised that at least 600-700 students were seated in that hall. I just got irritated for a while but then again I concentrated on her. Soon the class was over and we headed towards our van. I left with Ambar and Gautam and I don't know why I was feeling sad.

I was feeling a little bit insecure. Huh! Insecure? Insecure of what? And the answer was still a mystery. Was it Mishti or what? Why was I feeling insecure? I was in a fear of losing her, and the very next second I found myself talking to me, 'Idiot, fear of losing? Are you mad? How can you be afraid of losing something that is not yours?? WAAH!!!' I stood speechless and headed to van with them.

Firstly I decided to tell everything to her, that I don't know why but I think I am falling in love with you but I stepped back and relaxed myself; and got seated inside the van calmly. I was the first one to enter the van; Ambar and Gautam went to the very famous confectionary shop in kakadeo and that was 'ROCK n ROLL'. They went to eat something. I was sitting alone so I leaned back into the cushions and closed my eyes and relaxed and within no time my mind was lost in her thoughts. I quickly opened my eyes and thought, 'What nonsense is this??'

After 5-to-10 minutes Simmi and Kanika came and then Ambar, Gautam, Yudy and Arjun but Mishti was still missing; driver uncle asked us to call her and tell her to come quickly but we had not exchanged our numbers yet so it was not possible. We waited and waited and I was getting impatient and finally I stepped out of the van and my left foot was still in the air when Simmi asked, 'Now where you are going??'

I patiently replied, 'just to the coaching to look for Mishti...she has not yet came na...that's why'

She smiled and said, 'Then go na, for whom are you waiting... go'.

I went and had hardly walked 3-4 steps when I saw her coming, I stopped there and for at least 10 seconds I kept staring her, she had unpinned her hair and they were dancing with the wind and I also wanted to dance with the hair....she looked extremely beautiful in her purple top, and it perfectly suited her very very fair complexion. Suddenly I heard Arjun shouting, 'Bro if you are done then let us go'.

It felt like someone woke me up from my dream and I replied, 'Of course bro, just coming'.

I again got myself seated and waited for her to come. 'Sorry sorry sorry sorry!! I am late, but am I very late?' she asked breathing heavily.

I couldn't control myself and said, 'Arey no... It is okay'.

Although it was getting late but I still supported her and everybody smiled but the very next second they gave me a look that can scare the devil out of anyone. I just pretended as if I didn't know anything.

For some time there was a silence in the van when finally I spoke, 'Hey! Why you all are sitting so silently? I don't like these uncomfortable silences'.

Then someone taunted me in a very soft tone but I heard it and it was, 'Haan...like we all are here to entertain you.... as if we don't have any other work'

I ignored it and said, 'So Simmi, from which school you are?'

She replied very quietly, 'RYVN and you?'

'Achaarya's Gurukul' I answered her. I further added, 'Actually me and Kanika both have joined this school this year only and before it I was in MMS(Mercy Memorial School)'

'Okay!! So Kanika, you were also in MMS before joining here?' she asked Kanika now.

'Nope.... I've changed a lot of schools... I started my schooling from MMS and then GPA and then SEC and now here' she answered.

'Okay!! Good' she put a full stop to the conversation now.

So it was the 2nd day of coaching and the van and we got to know about each other's schools. Ambar and Gautam were classmates of 'The Scholars' and so obviously they had a nice tuning. Mishti was from St. Andrew's House of Education. Since it was a long way to home we talked to each other so that we could understand each other. Then it was the time to exchange numbers, and Simmi seemed to be very frank and friendly so I thought to start with her only. Although it was quite awkward to ask any girl's number and that too the very next day of meeting but still I asked, 'Arey yaar Simmi, tell me your cell number....'

She looked perplexed, I thought she was not willing to exchange the numbers but hesitating a little she slowly slowly spoke out the ten digits, 'A-a-a-a-a-a......n-u-m-b-b-b-b-e-e-e-r-r-r-r....okay write it...' She gave us the number. 'Give me a miss call everyone'.

Then I asked for every one's number but now was the time I'd been waiting for, time to get Mishti's number and I asked, 'Mishti, what is yours?'.

What I heard was unexpected, she said, 'Why?' in a very troubled look. I just felt embarrassed but I replied, 'Yaar We all should have each other's number just in case we need to contact...if you don't want to exchange numbers then it's perfectly alright'.

'Arey it's not like that....Okay' she replied and told her number.

And then finally we arrived home and me and Kanika said bye to everyone and stepped out of the van.

I entered the home and after having my dinner, I tried to revise the notes and solve some of the questions but I was not able to concentrate, one question was dancing in my head, 'I've seen Mishti somewhere before and not only once but I'd seen her 4-5 times and near the house..... I am 100% sure that I'd seen her before but I cannot remember......'

After thinking a lot, I got back to work and solved the questions. When I went to sleep, a sudden and random thought of her struck me and I remembered that I'd seen her in a nearby coaching institute for 10<sup>th</sup> class and also I'd seen her on my way to my previous school.

'Yes, she used to go to school riding a bicycle with her friends...Whatever, but I used to like her since then only.' I spoke it in my thoughts and finally fall asleep with a smile on my face.

That smile was obvious; I hope you all will understand why it was obvious especially those friends will surely understand who have ever been in a relationship.

# Chapter Ten

Never before, I'd such a peaceful sleep, a sleep with so much relaxation and a sleep with no worries of tomorrow. It was a beautiful and a carefree sleep like that of a baby. It seemed like I'd been waiting for this kind of sleep only and waiting from months. it was 4th of June, the 25th marriage anniversary of my dear parents. I got down from the bed and felt very fresh as if that day's morning was just different and brand new. Anyways I touched the feet of my parents and wished them a on the successful completion of these beautiful 25 years and prayed for this journey to become much more beautiful for them. After reading the headlines, I went to brush my teeth. Getting over with it I went for breakfast, the breakfast seemed really delicious, of course it should be, *and after all it's the 25th anniversary, not a joke.* On the dining table I could see Chinese, Italian, South Indian and few other dishes, they appeared very yummy! The best part was, they all were cooked by Mom so they have to be the best!!

Soon I finished my breakfast and the clock still showed 9:30. The time was passing very slowly and I had no other work to do except then to just waste it! I walked here and there in the whole house, sometime I went to the kitchen then the next minute I could be seen in the drawing room, then in the bedroom, then somewhere else and then somewhere else. I was getting so restless but somehow one hour passed and it gave me a little feeling of relaxation. Everything was so perfect that day that I found myself in a mental state of confusion, on the first thought I wished for the time to stop but the very next second I wanted the clock to show 3:00 pm, I didn't know what was happening but somehow I diverted my mind and went to a barber's shop to groom myself. I wanted to look very well organised that day as a great celebration was organised in the hotel that day.

'Yaar give me a clean shaved look...and clean means clean... and also trim some hair' I instructed the barber.

'Okay!' he replied.

It took me around 20-to-25 minutes to get a nice groomed look, I paid him and went back home and I realized that yes; I was looking kind of cool in short hair. I immediately took a bath and dressed myself as per the occasion. I saw the clock, it still showed 1 p.m.

'Why the hell is clock running so slow?? Anyways I should have my lunch and it is going to be 3 O' clock soon' I thought.

I sat down for the lunch and soon I heard, 'Hehehehe!! You duffer.... why did you get ready so early? Gone mad or what?'

It was Kanika.

'You just do your own work...have lunch if you want to and get ready'

'Arey everything is fine except the fact that since when you've joined the coaching, in fact since when you've joined the van...you are very happy?? What is the real inside story, *haan? Bandar ki tarah uchalte firtey rehte ho ghar bhar me. kyun?* Tell now....'

I thought now she knows everything, after all, she is my twin sister. For one second, I got much tensed that now what to tell her, how to share it with her and all those random thoughts kidnapped my mind. I don't know why but it is only shown in movies that brother-sister bond is so strong but in reality brother-brother and sister-sister bond is much stronger than it. If I had a twin brother, I would have told him but how to tell her.

*Who knows that if I had a twin brother then maybe he had also started hitting on Mishti... it's good that I've a sister!!!*

'Arey! You are really an irritating personality...why are you thinking so much?? Just tell me'

'It is nothing...Are you mad?? If you are hungry then eat the food not my head and now get lost' I replied like I didn't care about what she asked.

'Okay... don't tell but what do you think that I don't know anything?? I am aware of everything *bhai*....'

'Oh really? So if you already know then why are you dancing on my head? Just go and have lunch...mummy..... call her...she is disturbing me'

'Kanika, leave him and eat your food' mom shouted from the kitchen.

'Coming Mummy.'

'Okay okay... I am going...why did you call Mummy? Are you a girl?? She said and left singing, *'Badle badle se mere sarkaar nazar aatey hai, barbaadi ke aasaar nazar aatey hai'*.

Finally, it was 3 pm and I heard the same pattern of horn from the distance. I knew it was my coaching van and it gave me a reason to smile, and that was Mishti. I was dying to see her. I had this feeling for the very first time and

I just didn't want that feeling to go anywhere. For the first time, it happened that I waited eagerly for something.

The van stopped in front of my gate and I was so happy but I controlled my expressions and it was a surprise to me also that I was on time, in fact before time. I got inside and found myself a seat.

However I wanted to sit next to her but never mind.

'Where is Kanika?' asked Simmi.

'She is coming'.

She came after few seconds and the van started. I took out my ear phones and put them in my ears and started listening to one of my favourite songs, 'New Divide' by Linkin Park. I could see everyone lips moving but could not hear anything. Whenever I got a chance, I just watched her; I didn't want to miss any chance to see her.

At one time I had an eye contact with her and I felt very embarrassed, I quickly changed my view, and pretended as if I was trying to see something else but accidentally had an eye contact.

But something said inside me, 'Why are you feeling embarrassed...it may be possible that she must be watching you'.

I finally took those earphones out as I wanted to talk to her but each time something pulled me back. I was not able to summon that courage that was required to start the conversation. I could hear everyone talking but she was quite, she didn't talk much. Within no time we were at the coaching gates. We all stepped down and walked towards the building.

'Bro....it is the right time...go ahead... don't act like a *fattu*...just go man...she is going all alone....go and talk... accompany her dude' Yudy urged me on.

'Wait...what are you talking about? Why should I go and accompany her?'

'Bro... Please stop acting and start reacting....you think that we don't have eyes?? We have known you hardly from 2-3 days but we have known you quite well' Ambar said.

'Dude...true love cannot be hided from anyone....it can be clearly seen in the eyes...' Gautam added. They all pushed me and shouted from behind the van, 'Mishti.... Wait'.

I didn't know what to do now. She turned and smiled and said, 'Yes Kavya, What happened?'

Now what was I supposed to say, I smiled, hesitated, stumbled and I just picked up any random thought, 'Nothing... I just thought that you are going alone so why not to join you....just for the sake of company'.

'Oh! That's very sweet of you, come na' she kindly replied.

As we started walking I just closed my eyes, gained some confidence and courage and reopened them. We just walked and didn't utter even a single word. On stairs also, we just walked together.

At the entrance of the hall, she said, 'Thanks for your company, I enjoyed a lot, you speak a lot!!! Do something about it and ASAP'. I was happy for her kind words but then I realised she taunted me, of course she should. I was the one who offered her company and then I didn't speak a single word, how foolish of me yaar!!!

But I was happy for one thing and that was at least I got a topic to start with. 'Phewww!!! At least I overcame with my shyness today...' I said to myself and smiled. I then concentrated on the lecture and after that lecture we all went to the next coaching. After few hours both the coachings got over and we went all went back to the van.

I could not believe that I was late again; everyone was already sitting in the van when I got there. I was thinking of something solid to say, a genuine reason so I said, 'Are sorry yaar but I just went to buy a recharge coupon'

'It is okay dude...it is nothing new...just come inside' shouted Arjun.

I got in and sat down. 'Uncle, please stop the van at Agra Sweet House today' requested Yudy.

'Why? Do you have some work there?' I asked him.

'No...Absolutely not.... today I just wanted to share the famous *momos* with you guys' he answered.

'Really??' Simmi could not believe what she heard just now. She loves these stuffs like pizza, momos, chocolates and all. She is a great lover of all this.

The van stopped and we enjoyed those delicious *momos* and the credit goes to Yudy. Thanxx for that, man!!!

Mishti didn't eat even a single piece, we also did not insist much. Finally, when we came home me and Kanika said bye to everyone, and I especially said it to Mishti. She smiled and waved her hand, blinked her eyes and said bye, without any sound, she just used her lips not her voice. I just can't tell you how pretty she looked then.

After changing the clothes, I texted Mishti, 'Hey!!' I was pretty sure that I'll not get any reply but to my surprise, within two minutes my cell beeped and I opened the text with my fingers crossed. 'Hey!!' it was a reply from Mishti. I was so very happy that in a hurry I just replied her without any text, yes, and a blank message!!

'What is this??' she replied.

Now how could I tell her that it was all the result of super excitement and happiness? Anyways, I thought for a while and replied, 'Arey nothing, just by mistake'

'Okay! So how did you remember me today?' she replied.

Before I could write any reply she again sent me a message saying, 'BTW were you serious today in accompanying me? or it was just *aiwai?* I mean did you really want that or someone forced to do that.....' I didn't think of her questions but I thought *I must admit that her typing speed is very fast... here I am still writing the text and there she has already sent me two messages....!!!!!*

Then finally we chatted for at least one hour....

**Me:** Yaad ki baat nahi hai, bus aise hi socha thodi jaan pehchaan badhaayi jaaye and yes awaaz maine khud di thi and yaar aise mat kiya karo....questions pure likha karo, ye dot dot dot dot dot ka kya matlab hota hai?

**Mishti:** kk... are ye ek tarah ki style hoti h baat krne ki msg k thru... tumhe itna b ni pata?

**Me:** yup!! Nahi pata, m new to dis msging world.....

**Mishti:** kk..... so van me to bot shaant rehte ho? Kyu? Apni behan se darte ho???

**Me:** arey nahi.... kaha yaar kitna toh bolta hu, ha bus tumse nahi baat karta tum hi nahi baat karti...n mai darta varta nhi hu kisi se....

**Mishti:** Exactly.....mujhse baat nahi karte....mai baat karne layak nahi kya? Hehehe, just kidding....

**Me:** hehehe....tum bhi toh nahi karti...

**Mishti:** okkk.... chalo abse karungi....kalse...

**Me:** okay!!! I've heard that you are from Lucknow?? And here u r staying in ur relative's home....????

**Mishti:** ek baat toh hai tum ladko ki... baat bhale hi naa karo par baate badi jaldi pata lagwa lete ho?? Kyu?? Chakkar kya hai??? Hmm? Itna interest kyu ki baate pata lagwaane lage?? Mamla kya hai??

I got l'il worried and kind of scared... I felt that my image will be spoiled infront of her...

**Me:** arey sorry yaar!!! Dun take in the other way....m just asking, just for the sake of asking...... koi chakkar nahi hai.... mujhe toh bus sunne ko mila driver uncle se so I was just confirming.....

**Mishti:** hehehehe!!!! Ek baat aur bhi hai tum ladko me, ki koi ladki zara sa bhi direct ho jaaye ya tone change kar de to ghabra jaatey ho!!! Hehehehe....... chillaxxxxx!!!!!!! I was just kidding and I didn't take it in ne odr way... tumne kon sa way socha tha??? ;)

**Me:** Arreyyy!!!

**Mishti:** hehehehe....okay...no more kidding around... yup I'm from Lucknow and here m staying in my maasi's home. Actually Lucknow me IIT-JEE ki bahot achchi coachings ni h...so m in Kanpur.... any more questions ACP Kavya??? :p .....

**Me:** okay!! Kaafi achche se jaanti ho ladkon ko??? Chakkar kya hai?? Mamla kya hai?? And ACP??? Hehehe!!! No no... no questions ma'am..... u r free to go..... ;) u r very funny....lagti nhi ho but ho....

**Mishti:** Hehehe.... meri hi dialogue mujpe maar rahe ho?? Sharm nhi aati???Yahi to trick hai... jo dikhta hai wo hota nahi aur jo hota hai wo dikh bhi sakta hai aur nahi bhi...:p anyways leave this, tum itna kam kyu baat kar rahe ho?? I mean m toking more than u.... m cracking more jokes than u... r u a serious kind of guy??? Or just pretending in front of me?? ;) Ya hamesha aise hi rehti ho?

**Me:** arreyy nahi nahi.... m not a serious guy... bus thodi ajib lag raha hai na ki kya baat karu pehli pehli baar.... kuch samajh ni aa raha hai na.... ☺.

**Mishti:** oh!! U r truly a limited edition!!! Ladki ho ke mujhe ni itna odd lag rha ya ajib lg rha par tumhe lag rha hai... kbhi koi ladki friend nahi rahi kya???

**Me:** arey rahi hai par fir bhi....

**Mishti:** okay!!! Gud then... but please never ever offer ur company 2 sum1....

**Me:** oh!!!☹ Hehehe.... ya I just got nervous... smjh ni aaya ki kya baat karu...

**Mishti:** kk.... I can understand... so r v friends???

*Yes!!!! That was the question I was waiting for so long... finally......*

**Me:** Of course!!! Still any doubt?? ;) Its my pleasure....

**Mishti:** ☺ I guess v'll both enjoy this new f'ship n each other's company... okay now I've to go... gunnyt...swt drmzzz and tk cr... ☺

**Me:** Ya, u said very true.... Gunnyt Sd...Tc☺ c u 2mrrw...

# Chapter Eleven

Next morning was again the same, the same routine till 3pm and the same rate of heartbeat... as the clock's hour hand came closer to 3, I don't know why but my heart beat increased by itself. I closed my eyes for a while and opened it; it gave a feeling of calmness. I just closed them, didn't even think of anyone, I don't know why old people keep on saying that *ankhe band karne se dil halka ho jaata hai...* they don't have any scientific explanations but yes, it worked for the time being.

Like every day, the van honked its extra special horn "Po-po po-po-po po-po po-po-po". We (me and Kanika) went out and entered the van. That was something new; we all had an extra energy and a positive vibe... we all met and greeted each other very loudly and clearly. 'Hi' said Simmi and the very next second it was raining 'HIs' inside the van.

*I turned towards my heart, no no, not that in the left side, my heart was sitting in front of me, Mishti.*

I said 'Hi' with a spark in my eyes and a broad smile on my lips. 'Hey' replied she and smiled. Now I thought of what to say so that I could start a conversation, I just looked at her and I guess she was also thinking the same.

Somehow I managed to arrange a topic for myself. I started with, 'What message you sent to me yesterday... It was an incomplete message'

(*Although we finished the chat in a proper way with no incomplete messages but then also I said that just for the sake of speaking, so that she could reply and I could chat with her even more, like it is said* **'Baat karne se hi to baat banti h'**)

'Which message??' I didn't send any incomplete message' she replied.

(Yes!! *It worked; it totally worked as I planned*)

'Arrey! It was...anyways, leave it' came the swift reply from my side. 'Hmm' was the reply from her. Then again I was blank, I wondered what to say now? Just then Kanika played a song on her mobile, I don't remember which song was that but it really helped me a lot in some or the other way.

'Hey, is this song sung by the band American Idiot?' Mishti queried.

'No, you missed it just by that much. American Idiot is not any band, it's the song sung by the band Greenday' I replied like I was the only one who had the knowledge of English songs.

*I felt little proud of myself.*

'Oh haan, I meant that only' she defended herself.

Just then my cell phone rang, it was Lavanya calling. I received her call and said, 'Yes Lavanya....yaar I am on my way to coaching... if it is not so important then shall I call you after 8?'

After a pause I again said, 'Yes...hmmm...definitely... ok...call you at 8....bye.'

As soon as I hung the call, I received a text and it was surprising that why a person sitting right in front of me would text me, it was from Mishti. Before reading it I looked at her and gave her an expression of asking what it was.

She calmly replied from her eyes, her eyes said to read the message. I opened the text, it said, 'Who's Lavanya?? *Haan*?? Tell?? Tell?? What's the matter?'s

I smiled and looked up and smiled again at her and nodded my head and replied back, 'Why? Are you feeling jealous?? She is...sum1 spcl'.

This time she smiled and nodded and replied, 'Why would I be jealous and that to jealous of sum1 who I don't know....in your dreams dear...in ur drmzzz... hehehehe...!!!'.

I smiled again and replied, 'Oh! Sum1 has turned green with jealousy.... koi nhi...' Reading this she kicked me from her seat and unfortunately she missed me and poor Arjun became the target.

('*Oh boy!!!*' *I thought*).

Thankfully he didn't react but Mishti thought she hit me and I also didn't react so this time she hit even harder and this time her foot found the right target and that was me. I just shouted 'Aaaaah'.

'What happened?' asked Arjun and then answered, 'Oh!! So that was for you, good then....'

'Are leave yaar' I replied. Everyone was fully aware of what was happening in the van that day but they all ignored.

We attended the class and concentrated hard on the topic. The clock showed 6 pm and our great genius Mr. Ajay Vishwaas said in a very calm accent, 'Class dismissed!'

*That was super cool!!!*

We all rushed from the building and it was like a huge chaos there so I waited for sometime as I am very much afraid of crowds. I guess I was the last one to get out from that hall.

I was in the middle of stairs when my mobile rang and it was Mishti, I received her call and before I could even say 'Hello!' she asked, 'Where are you?'

'Just coming downstairs...you tell...need something?' I asked.

'Are nothing, I was waiting for you, so I thought that today I will give you a company...hehehehe.....' she replied.

*It was like a dream come true...*

'Okay! Wait, I am just coming'

*I hurriedly ran down from the stairs and even skipped few by jumping off them and within seconds I was at the main gate.*

She was waiting for me and was looking very beautiful like always, she was standing alone and she looked at her watch and then here and there for me. She looked beautiful with those looks and it was so lovely to realise that she was waiting for me; it gave me so much happiness that I stood still for some time and just kept looking her. It was the best thing to see someone waiting for you so eagerly as if you mean a lot to him or her. Truly, love is the best feeling in the life and perhaps the best thing. I was realising this day by day as I was getting more and more close to her. Gradually my bond was getting stronger with her.

I was lost in my thoughts when someone gave me little jerk, she was again Mishti and she shouted, 'Does it take 20 minutes to step down a few stairs? And from the last 5 minutes, I am waving my hand and you couldn't even see that? Lost in your own world, seriously you are pagal...'

'Sorry yaar!!' I said and smiled and bowed my head like a gentleman. I'd seen this gesture in some movies so I thought of applying it in real and it really worked, earlier I thought that this all shit worked in movies only like bowing your head in front of the girl and staying calm and smiling but it actually worked.

The very next second she smiled as if she never went mad at me just few seconds before. It seemed like she forgot all the anger and just smiled and said, 'Koi nahi yaar, it's okay!!'

'So you got late?' she added

'Arey yaar you'll laugh but then also I will say, I was late because I am afraid of heavily crowded areas, so I waited for the people to go, I am seriously very much scared of mob'.

As I thought she laughed and then controlled it, 'Oh! And what else are you afraid of??' and she started to laugh again.

I made an annoying face and started walking and ignored her.

'Arey sorry sorry, I didn't mean that yaar, sorry'

'Okay! So? Boys don't have a right to fear something? Everyone has some kind of phobia... I am afraid of blood... height and crowd....you laugh... I don't care but I am afraid of these things. And now if you want to come then come otherwise keep standing' I replied her in a very rude tone.

She felt sad and started walking with me; we didn't talk to each other on the way to van. I also felt that I overreacted and felt sad.

When I came back home, the first thing I did was that I texted her, 'I am extremely sorry yaar, I should not have shouted at you, sorry!! Please forgive me'

She didn't reply.

I texted few more messages but none of them were replied, even the rings of my calls fell on deaf ears.

I was very unhappy, and I was not able to think of anything, I copied many sorry messages from the internet but none of them helped me out of this. I laid down on the bed and kept thinking of how to change her mood but I couldn't think of anything.

'What happened bro?' asked Kanika.

'Nothing...listen...like if you had a small fight with your friend who is a boy then how do you both come back?'

She was completely blank because of my question, it was obvious, and anyone would become blank at this point.

'What are you trying to ask? I mean out of nowhere why you are asking this?'

'Nothing.... I was just asking for the sake of asking... actually one of my friends was asking me so I thought you can help' 'I don't know...sorry I can't help him but you listen idiot.... don't take tension and calm down...Mishti will be alright by tomorrow...'.

'Mishti!!! Where did she come from? I was telling about Kshitij... he was asking it.'

'Dont try to act smart...I am your twin sister... just sleep now...and if she matters to you a lot then why the hell did you shout at her??

'How'd you know that I shouted at her?'

'Why? Are you the only one who talks to her? She texted me and said I should not have laughed at Kavya, he became so angry'

'She could have texted the same thing to me also....?' I said in a confused way.

'Please....you don't know girls, she will be alright by morning and just go to sleep now and let me sleep'

'Are you sure? I confirmed one more time.

'Yup!! 100%, and now if you will utter a single word then I'll un tune your lovely guitar...good night...' She threatened me and went to sleep.

'Okay okay!! Good night.' I replied and went to sleep.

I knew that I would not be able to sleep but then also I tried and waited for the morning.

# Chapter Twelve

I woke up next morning at 11 am and the first thing I did was I checked my mobile, I was in a hope of her name in the message section but I was completely shocked to see 4 missed calls from Lavanya. Then I remembered that I was supposed to call her the previous day and I forgot. I put my hands on my face and just shouted in a low tone, 'Oh God!!'

I called back Lavanya and started with a sorry.

As expected she said the same, 'Someone was supposed to ring me at 8 yesterday....'

'Sorry..... I forgot and now am I allowed to speak? I asked gently.

'Of course... speak'

'Actually I could not sleep the last night so I slept in the morning....phone was on silent mode....so could not respond to your calls....'

'Oh ho!! Nice..... It seems that you also got someone to talk with whole night... who's the lucky one?' she pulled my leg.

'Are you mad?' I pretended as if I didn't know what she was talking about.

'Oh yeah... now you will not understand it, I know when you are making it up and when you are faking it... so just tell me.....are you in love...??'

I thought that whether what is the case, nothing can be hid from these girls.

'Okay you are right as always, okay her name is Mishti'
'See, I told you' she expressed her joy.

Then I narrated her full story of the last 3-4 days, how I met Mishti and that I liked her and everything. Lavanya expressed her happiness for me and comforted me with her kind words. We talked for around 40 minutes and when I hung up than I saw 3 new messages from Mishti and thanks to my dear sister; the replies were somewhat similar to what she told me.

Those messages gave me a new energy and I took a sigh of relief. That moment I realised my biggest fear and that was the fear of losing her. I closed my eyes and thanked the almighty!

In the evening I said sorry again in front of her with the same gesture by bowing down the head.

*(Seriously that bowing down of head was fun :P)*

'Arey! It's okay!! I am not upset with you yaar.... and you can stop bowing down your head... I don't look so much scary that you always have to talk like this....hahahahaha'

I was very much relaxed but this was my first fight or rather misunderstanding with her, that very moment I promised myself to never ever fight with her again, not because I could not win but because this small fight taught me a lesson and that was, one should control his anger, especially in front of that person who means a lot to him. One should not give up on something he cannot go even a day without thinking about.

*Within no time days passed away and we all became even better friends, our bond strengthened, we all were kind of a family now, we fought, we laughed, we cried at times, we became angry at others, we shouted, we screamed but in the end we loved each other. We stood there for each other in need, we helped each other, although we all were preparing for a competition yet we never let that feeling come among us, we were friends, infact best friends instead of being competitors. We enjoyed each other's company very much, we shared our emotions, and it was like we all lived together under a same roof from many years. We understood each other so well.*

Days converted into months. My bond with Mishti became very very strong. We used to chat all night, in coaching, in van and whenever we got time.

Our schools got re-opened and we'd to adjust our time between schools and coachings. It was a hectic and tiring schedule yet we didn't let our friendship to stand still, we managed and managed well.

My relation with Mishti was of a good friend until the month of October when something happened that brought us closer. Like old days we were returning from coachings and it was for the second time I sat next to her in the van, that day she looked a little down.

'Is everything alright? Are you okay?' I asked.

'Yes, absolutely fine' she replied.

Her eyes seemed to be in an argument with her tongue, they were so red and drowsy, and definitely something was wrong.

'*Sach batao, lag toh nahi rahi ho?*' I asked again.

Then without uttering a single word, she laid her head on my shoulder and said, 'Not feeling well, headache!!' and she almost slept.

That moment when she hid herself in my arms was like one of the best ones. It was a beautiful feeling to watch her resting her head on my shoulder and sleeping. I didn't want to disturb her sleep, so I didn't move, even in jerks I tried not to move.

She was sleeping so carelessly, I kept watching her and that moment was the best moment of my life till that day. For the first time I realised how it felt to be so close to someone who means the entire world to you, I just wished the time to stop, everything was so perfect that day, it just added to the moment.

For that 40 minutes I held my world in my arms, I felt like an angel was sleeping in my arms and I wanted to capture that moment but somehow I couldn't do that.

It was just for a second that I looked around the van as there was so much silence and then I found that each and every eye was on me and Mishti at that moment; even Yudy who always sits in front was turned back and looking at us.

I softly asked, 'What?'

No one replied but they just gave me smiles; none of them spoke for the whole time as they also didn't want to disturb her sleep. For this I will always be thankful to them.

Simmi said very softly, 'Nice Kavya, Good Luck' and smiled.

After sometime I found my hand in Mishti's hand. She held it tightly as if she was watching a bad dream and held my hand just to ensure that someone is with her always.

Now what to say this time, I just felt so good that I blushed in front of my van mates. Truly, that was the best feeling I ever had. Whenever she moved her head, I became still.

It was the same feeling like when someone holds a baby. Similarly, it gave me sense of responsibility towards her, in a second I was a bit more matured, it felt like now I had to be more sensible and practical and now I had someone for whom I had to look after. The feeling of care grew by itself. My love got multiplied and my tensions were divided or rather vanished. Now only she was in my head.

Fear of losing her developed within me, she was so ignorant, so innocent, how could I let anyone hurt her, how could I let her cry, how could I let her go, how could I fight with her, how could I lose her, these were the questions revolving in my head. And the answer was common and that was I couldn't afford to lose her.

There was a railway crossing in the way to home and most of the time it remain closed and so it was that day. I also closed my eyes for a while and I found myself walking in a heavenly atmosphere like a paradise, and the best part was I was walking with Mishti holding her hands but soon I woke up and noticed that I was still in the van. *It was so filmy!*

Soon I realised that she was in a deep sleep and it seemed that she was really not well so I didn't disturbed her which I was going to do at first thought. I thought that why she chose my shoulder when Tanya's shoulder was available on the other side and this was the thought that made me to think that she also liked me somewhere in her heart.

Then the moment came that I hated sincerely, that was of going home and stepping out of the van. Everyday van used to stop at my home before stopping at her's. That day due to of some traffic problem, uncle took another route and her stop was first in that route. She was asleep, I didn't want to wake her but what to do, I had to do that evil thing and I did, I woke her 2-3 times, she looked really weak.

'Are you feeling better?' I asked.

She nodded which meant half yes and a half no.

'We are home... step down...carefully'

She was not able to stand and walk so I stepped out of the van and helped her in coming out of the van by lending my hand. I was standing out, therefore I helped her walk; I supported her and took her inside her home. I'd just entered the home when her maasi came running and I handed over to her from there. She looked much tensed after watching Mishti.

'What happened? Is she okay??' she queried.

'Of course she is... just a little headache and all' I answered.

'Thank you son'

It was so nice of her, her maasi seemed very gentle and kind. It was the first time I'd met her.

'Please Aunty don't embarrass me. Good night'

'Good night Mishti, take care' I added and went back to the van.

Now the silence of the van was shattered by the screaming of Ambar, Arjun and Yudy, 'W-o-o-o-h-h-h-h-h!!!!! Party!!!! Party!!!'

I understood and smiled and said, 'Are you guys mad? Here someone's head is paining and you all are partying?? Such a shame!!!'

'Oye...shame?? For what?? We are just happy for you... and we just got to see a romantic scene...hahaha...now give us a party' Simmi and Kanika said together.

'Acha Kavya, why don't you tell her that you love her?' asked Simmi.

'I must tell you that living under the burden of such feelings is not a good idea, you will not be able to walk for long under this burden, either you tell her or stop thinking about her and I guess the second option is very much difficult.... so why don't you just tell her' she added to her question.

'Hmmm. Good question...but the answer is that I am afraid of losing her... I fear that I will lose her even as a friend...and when people are confident enough to hear a yes from the opposite side, even then they are afraid of expressing their feelings and I am confident enough of hearing a no'

'Okay... but today I felt...in fact everyone of us felt that she has a soft corner for you.... you must approach first... because guys approach first...it's my personal and friendly advice... else your wish boy..!!!!' she advised me.

'May be she is still not aware of this fact but she will get aware and I am 1000% sure about it... okay then whatever you decide just make sure that it is good for you....' she added.

'Yup!! Thanks for your friendly advice... I'll remember it.'

Then within few minutes, van stopped at my home and me and Kanika stepped out of the van, my happiness was clearly visible. I laughed at the gesture made by Ambar and said bye.

# Chapter Thirteen

More months passed away, life went on in the same old way like school, coachings and school and friends, new friends, old friends. Life kept revolving around these things only when winters arrived. This time winters were little special or I can say that I felt it like that. It was 25th December, Christmas and I was very happy as I've decided to propose Mishti that day.

Since it had been a long time to our friendship and I felt the closeness that was between us. It was something more than friends' type of a relation between us but we both were aware of it. It was not like that only I'd feelings for her, my heart had always told me that somewhere she was also inclined towards me but either she didn't admit it or she was still fighting with this thought. In the past few months, time and circumstances had brought us even closer to each other, we had known each other very well.

We were now more than just best friends, I'd feelings for her, I was not sure about her but the point was that I'd feelings for her and now I could not carry this burden of feelings any further. It was the time to take our friendship to a next level. I had decided a long time back that I would propose her on X-mas, as it is one of the most romantic festival types and also the weather stays calm and peaceful which adds to the beauty of the festival. It just mixes up some fragrances of romance in the air and sound of the romantic melodies with the *Jingle Bells*.

A fear prevailed inside me and that was what would happen if she said a big "NO". Fear ran down my whole body just by this thought. Fear was not of being rejected, it was of what if she finishes the extra special friendship. What if my proposal hurt her, what if she considered me only a friend?

The fear was mounting up gradually but I'd decided that whatever the outcome be, I would not step back now. I would propose and that was final and certain.

If she was destined to be mine, no one could stop it.

Everything was set but the question was how I would propose her, it requires a lot of courage to propose someone. It's not a child's play. It's even complex and difficult than solving Mathematics. I was nervous and didn't know how to get a pick up line, I Googled but couldn't find something new or special. Then like always I went to Kanika and said, 'I am going to propose Mishti today'.

She was combing her hair and getting ready for the coaching and suddenly she dropped the comb as if I'd said something that I was not supposed to say.

'What!!! Really???' she asked in a shock.

'Yes and now tell me how to do it? Just tell me a good and romantic pick up line...if you know?'

'I don't have any pick up line brother...but I can help you... in the evening...we'll go to the church...there you can serve your purpose...and believe me proposing in the church is the second most romantic place for such a purpose....I'll tell everyone via message' It was helpful.

'Okay but what is the most romantic?' I inquired.

'Leave it... that is out of your budget...hahahaha'

'Just tell...'

'Okay...it's proposing just under the Eiffel Tower in France...'

She messaged everyone in the van except Mishti about my proposal and that in the evening we would go to the church.

Arjun and Yudy were absent that day. I was waiting for the coaching to get over. Soon the class dismissed and as planned, we all requested uncle to take us to any nearby church. He agreed and took us to the most famous church nearby named 'St. Xavier's Church' in Ashok Nagar.

It was a heavily crowded place that day, everyone came to visit Lord Jesus and so were we. For the first time in my life I went to a church. It was a very beautiful place and highly decorated that day. It seemed like a piece of heaven that accidentally fell on earth. We also entered the church, bought few candles and a match box and entered the premises of the church.

I don't know why I began to lose consciousness and sat on the bench for a while.

'What happened?' asked Gautam.

'Nothing bus I just want to sit for a while'

I guessed Mishti understood and said, 'Why did you come here? When you know you are afraid of mob and crowd?? You were not supposed to come... now hold my hand and walk slowly slowly' she said.

I held her hand and entered the main hall; we all lighted the candles, kneeled down and prayed. It is said that every wish on Christmas is fulfilled so I just asked for Mishti and nothing more.

I'd seen in movies people saying what it felt to walk in heaven with an angel but now I realised what it really felt and meant. Mishti was holding my hand, she was guiding my way and we were in the house of the God which was not less than any heaven and she is an angel. She stood quiet but then also her eyes were speaking a lot.

She fought for me when I didn't fight for myself. I was pushed by a man and I almost lost my balance but somehow managed. She shouted at that man, 'Are you insane? *aankhein hai ya button?*'.

It felt so very good that I didn't even care about the crowd, I just kept looking at her and suddenly everything became inaudible. Even her voice was not audible, I could only see her lips moving and her eyebrows rose at that man. I stood there and just saw.

Suddenly Kanika whispered in my ears, 'This is the right time...go ahead...go in that mini garden...best of luck'.

I was about say something when Ambar also whispered, 'Yup dude...just go...and I am sure you will make it man, I'd seen sense of insecurity and possessiveness about you in her eyes, *maa kasam sach bol raha hu*'

Gautam pulled me back and said, 'Bro... Good luck but also be prepared for a no.'

Now only Simmi was left to give advice. I turned towards her, 'Now you also want to say something?'

'Haa, Good Luck' she smiled.

Mishti shouted from behind, 'What you all are doing? Coming or not? And please any one try to make him understand...that don't walk alone. I've said to hold my hand but this is also not acceptable to him, *ekdam typical boys wala ego hai!!*'

'Okay...Okay...let's go!' I shouted.

'You both carry on...we will be there in just a moment' Simmi said.

'Okay! But come soon ha...' Mishti replied.

She looked at me and said, 'So...where to go?'

I looked here and there and said, 'Hey...there...that is something garden type...it looks a peaceful place...'

'Hmmm' she agreed.

We both entered the garden and sat on the bench made there. Surprisingly there were only we two human beings. Somewhere inside I felt happy that it will serve my purpose. That night was so romantic, never ever it had been so beautiful, it seemed as if it was waiting for this moment only to become so beautiful. Stars were twinkling and the moonlight directly fell upon that garden where we were seated, in fact it fell upon the garden only and everywhere else, it was completely dark.

It appeared as if the moon also wanted to listen to what I had to say, stars gathered right above the garden in the sky to listen to me and suddenly I heard the sweet singing of the church's choir. They sang the very melodious Christmas songs. This all happened just within 15-20 minutes, I thanked it as I thought that they all, the moon, the night, the stars and the choir were somehow helping me. It gave me a little push and the atmosphere that was needed.

After almost 20 minutes of chatting and giggling with her, I thought not to waste any more time so I said, 'I want to say something and it's really important and no joke and I am damn serious'.

She became serious and said, 'Okay...say it'.

I summoned up the courage, my heartbeat increased a lot, I became nervous, IN A FULLY FILMY WAY, I got on my knees, held her hands but I said whatever I felt like, *'Listen, it may sound a little odd to you or may be funny but I want to admit that I am deeply in Love with you!! I can't lie but I love you a lot. I didn't believe in love at first sight until I saw you the very first day in the van. There are so many things that I have always wanted to say to you, but it is hard to find the right words. From the day I met you, I've been completely taken by you. It is not only your sweet scent that draws me close to you but also your kind heart. Every time I see you, it makes my heart leap with a joy. I'd be lost without you. I promise to love you forever, every second of forever. I promise to take care of you. I promise never to hurt you. I promise to love you and just you. I promise to devote my entire life in loving you. I love you, I will always do. You are the very best part of my life. You made my ordinary life a celebration. It is too easy to be myself with you. You are the best thing to ever happen to me. In the end I'd like to say that you'll always be my friend no matter what your answer is. I hope that this will not create a gap between us; I said so because it was becoming harder and heavier to move on under the load of these feelings. I can't lie to myself. I'll be waiting for your answer. I should be leaving now; we all will be waiting for you in the van'.*

I felt relieved and I left. At least I was free from the chains of these feelings. I was happy and sad at the same time, happy for having said what I wanted to and sad because of the thought of losing her and her friendship. I knew what I saw, I saw her face which looked totally surprised, it meant she never expected this from me and there was nothing from her side. She looked completely shocked.

I headed towards the van and on my way I thought, 'seriously, the church is so romantic and beautiful, no place can be better than this.' I was also not able to believe that it was me who said all this, WOW!! It is said exactly right that once you start something, courage to finish it and the strength required comes by itself.

I entered the van and was welcomed with a nonstop and never ending series of inquiry. They all successfully set up the chain reaction of their curious questions.

'How'd it go?' Simmi was the first one to ask the most obvious question.

'I don't know'

'Then also... you might have an idea or something?' asked Ambar.

'Yes... so what do you think?' this time Gautam asked.

'Just tell it. Don't be a V.I.P...No need to shy in front of us... Yes or no?' Kanika asked.

'Okay okay! I don't know...I just think I should never have done this... she looked completely troubled and shocked....I am feeling sad.'

'It's okay... Be positive... just chill and relax, give her some time to decide and till then, don't get to any conclusion. I am pretty sure that she'll accept your proposal', Simmi comforted me with her much needed kind words.

'Yup... just be positive' said Kanika.

'Hope for the best and be prepared for the worst' advised Gautam.

'Where is Mishti?' Kanika asked.

'Must be coming...and please don't talk any non sense please, okay?' I requested them.

'Okay!!' replied all of them.

Finally after 10-15 minutes she arrived looking down the ground as if she was in a deep thought process. We all could make out what she was thinking about. She entered the vehicle, but we didn't speak anything. She also pretended that they didn't know anything and said, 'Sorry, I got little late.'

She talked a little and put her head down on her lap and I guess she slept for a while. We all also talked through eyes. Ambar told me to ask her whether or not she is all right but I refused. Then Simmi asked her and the reply was not unpredictable.

Then I requested to leave her and let her relax. We also just talked for a while and then everyone just shoved in their earphones and left being interested in the matter. After few minutes, van dropped everyone of us to our homes.

Although I was at home now but I kept thinking about the evening, I was worried and also curious to know her answer but at the same time I was thinking of how to meet her the next day. I was very tensed and worried, worried what if my first loves remained incomplete? What if she says no, what if my friendship dies with this evening? That night was very long, it was not passing away, it just stood there, time stopped and my eyes were still open in the dark room.

I turned my head to talk to Kanika but she was in deep sleep. I turned back and continuously stared the ceiling, although nothing was visible yet I just stared it.

Soon I heard a voice, 'It is 6 am... Won't you go to the school?' She was my mother shouting at me.

I woke up and wondered that when I fall asleep. I got up and washed my face and I could see Mishti saying a no to me in the mirror. I hurriedly washed my face again and sat on the bed afterwards. After thinking for a while I decided not to go to school that day.

I told mummy that I am not going to school. She didn't ask any further questions.

Kanika went to school so there was no one to talk with so I called Ambar and asked, 'Are you going to school?'

'No...Why?' replied he.

'I want to meet...can you make it at 11 at Upper Crust's Bakery?' I asked again.

'Okay... see you at 11...' he replied.

'Okay...bye then' I replied and disconnected the call.

At 11:15, I went to the Upper Crust and Ambar also came around that time.

'Yes... you are looking troubled? What happened?' he asked.

'Just in tension buddy...'

'It is okay.... give her some time...she'll text you in some days...till then stay relaxed... and don't talk from your side as well...' He advised me like a typical Love Guru.

'And just tell me one thing... that why the hell did you fall in love with Mishti, I mean when you had a better option, Simmi... hehehehe… she looks hot man... Mishti is sexy but dude Simmi is steaming hot!! Have you ever noticed her curves? Incredibly curvy body....if only you mean what I am saying...hehehe.' He added and expressed his *horny* views.

'Have you lost it? Here I am trying to explain my situation and you are interested in a girl's figure? I asked for your advice and you are busy in *maalbaazi!* Bro, I am serious....just let it go' I shouted at him.

'Hehehehe.... okay.. don't be mad at me.... listen.... just be patient...and let her decide, and no matter if she refuses, you are not the king...but one thing I can assure you that she will be your friend like always..... Now stop thinking and let us eat something....'

'Two Jungle Sandwiches' he ordered to the man in the shop.

I processed his words and now finally relaxed; we ate the very famous sandwiches.

'By the way... you are right... my friends also say the same about Simmi...hehehehe... and I guess you people are quite right but only up to an extent...hahahaha' I said while eating the sandwich.

'*Tharki*, you are really a dog and that to a stray dog....' he laughed.

'*Bhow Bhow*....hehehe' I barked and we both finished the sandwiches.

Many days passed away in the same way, New Year also passed and it was nothing new for me. She didn't utter even a single word to me.

I left the hope and accepted that this was the end to this friendship but it should not have ended like this. I felt bad but moved on. The worst part of it was to face her everyday and fall in love with her everyday and what was even worse was that to face her with a sense of guilt that it was me who put a full stop to this friendship. Her eyes spoke that I should not have done what I did that evening.

I just lost all the hope and kind of adjusted to it. It was of 4th January of the New Year and her birthday was approaching. It was on 6th January. I'd planned many things for her, to make her birthday special but I myself ruined it.

# Chapter Fourteen

I spent one more day without talking to her, it was the night of 5th January and the clock showed 11:47 pm. I was in dilemma of whether to wish her birthday or not. I was continuously thinking that should I call her or text or should I do nothing. In front of my eyes was my mobile, on its screen only her name and number was visible. My thumb was on the green dial button and I was so scared to press it. Somehow I pressed it but the very next second I pressed the red button. I did this for 3-4 times then finally I opened the message section and wrote a beautiful message, 'Happy birthday dear!!! ☺'!! Again my thumb shivered in sending that text, I could not press that round button.

I closed my eyes, pressed it and kept the mobile aside. I didn't want to face it, I didn't want to read her reply, although I was more than sure that she would not reply yet I was scared. Actually I was scared of the fact of what would I do if she replies and the reply is harsh and bitter. The clock showed 12:25 pm and I didn't receive any message from her, this made me a little impatient and I called her without thinking. Call was connected in the very first attempt, I thought that at least it would take 2-3 attempts for me to connect to her as it was her birthday and she might be busy on phone. I was thinking this and was thinking of what to say when suddenly she said, 'hello!' in a normal tone.

'Hey happy birthday' I wished her and waited for her to reply.

'Thanks a lot' she replied.

Now it was my turn to say something so I asked, 'Who all wished? And you didn't reply to my message also?'

'Everyone did and you were the last one, and I am so sorry, I really dint see the message' she said.

I thought she seemed to be okay with me and I was making my own perceptions like that only.

'Are you okay? I mean are you still upset?'

'Still upset means?? I was never upset'.

'Oh... you were not talking from 10-12 days so I thought....'

'You were also not talking... don't blame me always... acha listen, I'll talk to you in the morning...just don't go to school... I've a plan and something really important to say'.

'Okay okay! But what about you? I mean your school friends must be waiting for a party from you?'

'No, I have still no good friends in the school...this city is new for me, this place, this school and school friends, everyone is new for me....I've already told everyone about this in the van...we'll enjoy tomorrow, watch a movie and then to coaching'.

'Okay okay!! Cool!! See you tomorrow then'.

'One more thing...van will not come tomorrow...we all have to come by ourselves... Don't be late as you always do...' she said.

'Okay!! I'll take the car tomorrow... I'll pick you up from home'

'No it's not required, if you want to come in your car then it's okay but I'll manage myself... you can come along with others'.

'Why? You don't have to go alone... if you will come with us, only then I'll come'

'It is not done... it is my birthday so you do not dare to argue... *tum kya tumhaare to farishtay bhi aayenge*'

'Okay...then take those *farishtay* only with you...I am not coming if you don't show up tomorrow at 10... You are coming with us.....'

'Okay okay! We'll see to it tomorrow morning....for now, bye and thanks again... good night and take care...'

'Good night, you too take care...' I said and disconnected the call.

I thought that 'It is good that she is behaving normally and I was worried like that only... *stupid me!*'

I smiled and went to sleep. I waited eagerly for the morning as now I can execute my plan that I'd planned for her birthday....

Although there was no time yet I had enough of it.

Next morning I woke up at 6 am and switched on the desktop and transferred all the pictures of her that I had, that I had captured during these 7-8 months, in a pen drive and waited till 9 am. Till then I finished my other works and as soon as the clock struck 9, I took the bike and went to the gift shop nearby, I was sure that I would found it open, and so it was.

I parked my bike and entered the shop.

'Take this P.D and create a beautiful collage of pictures which are in it.' I said to the shopkeeper.

'Sir, it will take at least two-to three-hours'

'Don't say this...please...you can charge extra money but please return it in an hour...it's an urgency dude.'

'Sir it is not possible, but I'll try'

'Okay...but please make sure...it is done.'

'Okay! Sir, you can take it at 10'

I thanked him and left for a barber's shop. It was nearby so I didn't have to search. I entered and thankfully there was no customer, I was the first one to enter. I quickly got myself a proper groomed look and left for home.

When I entered home, I heard dad whispering to mummy, 'What is today? Something special? *Babuji* is looking different...Kanika is also at home? What is the matter?'

I turned towards him and he pretended as if he had not said anything and fixed his eyes in the newspaper.

I also didn't leave any chance to have fun with him and said, 'Mummy, please ask someone to read the newspaper gently else...' and ran away laughing.

'*Aye*, Shut up and go' mummy ordered me. Dad ran after me and within no time it appeared that I and dad were playing *Pakdan pakdaayi*.

'Dad, Stop it...just read your newspaper, why are you behaving like a kid, mummy *d-e...d-e...d-e-k-h-o... a-a-a-i-i-e-e-e.. hehehehe...*' I said while running in the house.

I rushed into the bathroom and locked the door but I could hear the conversation between him and mummy.

'Hehehehe, Bring my tea' he said to mummy.

'Why do you always tease him?

'A father should be friendly with his children...you should also try it sometime....it is good to give them some time in their way'

I was listening this and burst into a laughter and shouted from inside, 'Why? Did you watch 3 Idiots yesterday?'

'You just come out then I'll tell you which movie I saw' he replied.

I laughed even more and started singing, '*Kon darta hai Papa se, kon darta hai Papa se...hehehehehe*'.

'Kavya, Just keep quiet' mummy intervened.

When I came out of the bathroom, dad was gone to office and it was about to be 10, I hurriedly dressed up and discovered that Kanika had already finished her breakfast and was ready.

'You Mr. *late lateef*' she expressed her deepest sorrow. :p

'Just shut up please, and take out the car' I kind of ordered her.

'I am not your driver'

'Huh! Okay! You are not the only one who knows driving...I'll do it myself...*Hatt!!*' I started a cold war with her while combing my hair.

'*Tu hatt!*'

'Just stop fighting...and who is this Mishti?' mummy again intervened between me and Kanika, that day I was so sure of winning that cold war but she saved her from getting defeated.

*Shucksss!!!*

'She is a van mate...Mishti **Mathur**...today is her birthday, so we are going for an outing sort of....and we'll straight away go to the coaching. Van will not come, so I am taking the car'

*I kind of emphasised on her surname just to indicate her that she was of the same caste!! Although, my parents don't believe in the caste system, yet I did that....just in case...!!!*

'Okay...but drive slowly and safely' mummy replied.

The doorbell rang and I was sure that it would be Mishti. I asked Kanika to open the door, 'Please open the door, must be Mishti'.

'You are such a hypocrite.... when you want your work to be done, and then you surprisingly turn so sweet..... I guess Simmi and the company must be there' she replied.

Yes! There was Ambar at the door.

I thought, '*It is rightly said by Rudyard Kipling that a woman's guess is much more accurate than a man's certainty*'

Soon everyone was at my home, except Yudy, Arjun and Mishti.

I called everyone else except Mishti and got to know that those two could not come because of some reasons, I was just going to call Mishti when she showed herself. She looked very beautiful as always but that day she had done extra special thing to her hair, she had curled her hair and that style suited her very much.

I welcomed her inside and I remembered about that collage. You all wait, I am coming in ten minutes' I said and took out the car. I swiftly drove it to the shop and almost died when I saw the shop was closed. I waited for 10 minutes when the shopkeeper arrived and said, 'I was waiting just for you sir...please take your P.D and collage.... I have something important work'.

After receiving that collage, I finally took a sigh of relief and thanked him. I paid him and with the same speed I drove back to home.

'Where were you?' inquired Kanika.

'Had some work' I answered.

Just then mummy entered with some snacks and I introduced everyone to her. She said, 'Kanika had already finished with the introduction, I want to meet the birthday girl'.

'Okay! So here is your birthday girl' I introduced Mishti to her.

'*Namastey aunty!*' she greeted mummy.

'Namastey beta, happy birthday'

'Okay okay... now we should leave... else we'll miss our movie' I reminded them.

'Yes, we should leave' Gautam said and we left for the movie.

I was driving very normally and safely when again Kanika said, 'Don't show off! Drive like a civilised person'. This time she really annoyed me and I slowed down to 30 Kmph.

'Have you gone mad? What are you doing? We'll miss the movie if you'll drive like this' shouted Simmi.

'What should I do? You people decide it first...' I shouted back.

'Don't get angry bro.... you drive in your style' Ambar said and turning towards them he said, 'Please let him drive in his own way...else you'll not be able to watch movie... don't you guys know him?'. He turned towards me and laughed and said, 'Drive dude...drive'.

I smiled and softly said, '*haraamkhor!*'. He laughed back.

Soon we reached our destination, and said, 'You all step out and I'll meet you guys up there in the hall'. I then parked the car and went directly to the movie hall where they were waiting for me. We entered the hall and found our seats. I wanted to sit next to Mishti but ould not sit. I sat next to Simmi and enjoyed the movie. After the movie was over we went to the food court.

The movie was not up to the mark but we all had a great time together. We enjoyed at the Domino's and did little shopping. Kanika and Simmi gifted Mishti a very beautiful top. I must admit that girl's sense of shopping and selection of clothes is far better than boys. I, Gautam and Ambar bought a delicious and a big chocolate cake for her. We made her cut that in the FC only. We also sang the song and enjoyed a lot. Every other eye was on us but who the hell cared! We captured some wonderful pics and soon it was 3:30 pm. It was time to attend the coaching.

At first I thought of bunking the lecture but then I had kill that thought as no one seemed interested in bunking the lecture.

'Let's go to the coaching now' I said.

'You drive the car to the main gate, we'll be waiting there' Gautam said.

'Let's walk... it is not so far...let the car be parked here. In the evening, we'll come back here' I explained them.

'Okay...' Simmi agreed and so did everyone else.

We started walking and soon we were in the classroom. After the class got dismissed, I walked out of the building and as it was decided I was waiting for others at the gate number 2 and then I saw Mishti approaching. After few seconds she also joined me and accompanied me in waiting for the others. I guess around 30 minutes passed away but there was no sign of them and then I received a call from Ambar saying that, We all are already in the mall, you come along with Mishti' and he disconnected the call.

'What happened?' asked Mishti.

'Nothing, they have already reached'

'Okay!! Let's go'

We had just started walking when she broke the silence by saying, *"Acha mera gift kaha hai?"*

I took that collage out from my bag and said, 'It is not so good but it is wrapped with love and our friendship and the eternal bond that we share, it may be ordinary for anyone but not for me... take this and *happy birthday*'

'Oh it's very sweet'.

She unwrapped the gift and it made her to smile after watching that. She smiled and looked at me and said, 'It's one of the best gifts I'd ever received. It's very beautiful and beyond words. Thank you very very much. I'll never lose it... it's very special, thank you once again...'

I smiled at her and suddenly she hugged me and screamed, 'T-h-a-a-a-n-k-k y-o-o-o-u-u-u s-o-o-o-o m-u-c-h-c-h-c-h!!! You really made my birthday very special'

I wondered what was happening and then she became normal and said, 'I actually wanted to talk to you about one more thing and that is about that Christmas eve and I wanted to talk to you in alone, finally I got to talk to you alone'.

I became very very nervous, my heartbeat was in a race with time I guess, it beat so rapidly. 'Okay!! Say it' I replied without looking at her.

'First of all, look into my eyes.... like you did when you proposed me...if you are afraid of facing the consequences, then why did you speak all that stuff? Just look into my eyes' she ordered.

I looked up and all I could see was anger, and anger.

'Okay okay... say it'

'Were you serious that evening?' she asked 'and reply me looking into my eyes' she added.

'What do you think?'

'I asked it first' she overruled my question.

'Okay yes I was dam serious.'

'Okay! I also thought you must be serious, okay listen now, I truly and sincerely respect your feelings but yaar...' she had said only this when I spoke in between, 'But I don't feel the same for you, I am sorry, we can just be friends and nothing more...oh yeah!! I know this thing...please tell me something new yaar'

'Finished? Now do not utter even a word? Either you speak or let me do so. Now just shut up and listen, listen well.... I sincerely respect your feelings and admire you but today we are not that much mature yaar, I mean we are just kids, we are hardly 16 or 17 and we have a lot of things to do, we have our boards of 12th approaching and then competitions and colleges... so I don't think this is the right time to fall into any relationship... I am not saying that I don't want to or it's you with whom I don't want to, I am just saying that I don't want this shit in my life.... please don't misunderstand me.. You have always been a good friend and will always be. This will never build any wall between the two of us... so just concentrate on studies, and let our parents find a perfect match for ourselves. *And kya pata mere parents tumhe ko dhund le... hehehehe...* chill now' she explained me quite dramatically.

Her last line was so much irritating, like had said it for fun but it was a taunt like just *Fuck off!!!*

I just nodded my head and we started walking again. I reached to the car parking. I drove the car to the main gate where they all were waiting and waited for everyone to settle down. After that I just drove very slowly and dropped everyone to their homes and then back to home.

I narrated her answer to Kanika and she also had no words of comfort. She said, 'It is okay. Don't be sad... she had not said a 'no'....calm down'. I called Yudy and asked for some suggestion but he also gave me the same advice.

I was heartbroken but I could not help it, I wanted to cry, wanted to scream but somehow I could not.

# Chapter Fifteen

It took me few days to adjust myself to the whole scenario set up by her and her diplomatic reply. For many days I kept wondering that what she actually wanted to say, was it a no or was it a future yes, I also thought that a girl should never give these kinds of replies which only increases the curiosity and tension, if it was a no she should have said it directly. What was the need to hang me in the middle of yes or no? Neither I could be happy nor could I mourn over my partial rejection. I just hated her once in my life time and that was for this reason only, for not giving a straight and a simple reply. *I was angry on her but still I loved her.*

One day in the coaching I realised that while I was busy loving her, I forgot that she was the most beautiful girl in the coaching and she had many admirers just like me, some were nice and good, some were quiet and calm, for some she was just an *eye candy* but some were seriously dangerous and illiterate type of people. Whole coaching was in love with her but I was the lucky one to have her. Every other boy died to talk to her, to see her and they waited whole day outside the building just to have a glimpse of her when class gets dismissed.

I also realised that I had made several foes for myself, and those were none other than her many lovers in and around that KAKADEO. They were envious of me; they wanted to like beat me seriously. They thought that she was my girlfriend and wanted that I should get off from their way. When I realised all these facts, it scared the hell out of me! I was completely scared, not because of the fact of getting into a dramatic fight someday but of the fact that she was now insecure. Second thing that I realised was in the whole area it was our sweet white Omni that was being targeted from few days. Ambar also realised this along with Gautam. It was the time when Arjun had changed his van as he wanted to go with his school friends and Yudy had left the coaching as he got fascinated of being an army officer, so he started preparing for that.

I first realised these both things when I saw boys capturing pictures of Mishti and making videos but I could not help it. How could I? I could not fight with around 300-400 boys out of which everyone is ready to like kill you! Then comes the thing of van getting targeted, it was also noticed the very next day when Mishti was captured. We saw 5 boys following the van on their bikes and they followed till the home. Firstly I thought that they just wanted to know the home of Mishti but I was wrong, they actually wanted to know the home of every girl in the van.

It was the mid of January when these all things started to get onto my nerves. I avoided it for the long time but this was the time when my patience gave up.

I was returning from my Maths coaching and near that 'Rock n Roll' confectionary shop Mishti was waiting for the van. I saw her and joined her.

'From how much time are you waiting?' I asked.

'Just 5 minutes... uncle took the van to fill her up' she answered.

'So can we drop?' somebody whispered from behind.

I turned around and saw a group of boys, and noticed that these were the guys who were following the van continuously from few days. I avoided them and called Ambar, 'Where are you?'

'On my way...with Kanika and Simmi'

Then I called Gautam and said him to come ASAP. I actually did all this for a safety reason, like it is said *Sanghathan me shakti hai aur akele me fatti hai.* It was true, I was kind of afraid as I was alone with her and I was sure of being getting smashed if I did anything.

Soon they all came and it gave a support, we waited for a while and then van also arrived. I took a sigh of relief!!

Next day I, Gautam and Ambar bunked the coaching and I discussed this fact with Gautam and Ambar. I said, 'Guys...are you noticing this all?? This following of the van and all this shit....I mean in whole area, they only see our van and my Mishti?'

'My Mishti!!! The answer is that our van is full of *maals*... whether it is Kanika, Simmi or Mishti...just avoid else we all will be beaten up someday.' Ambar said.

'Yes.... just avoid...else you will be the first one to be smashed... hehehehe' Gautam interrupted Ambar.

'True.... I am a thin fellow, and will be easily smashed up...hahahaha... and that's why you, Ambar just stay with me... you look so monstrous....hahaha'

While returning to the van at the time of coaching dismissal we decided to tell this to the girls.

Ambar started with, 'Listen, from tomorrow, we all will come together, don't ask anything, it's for everyone's safety...'

'The reason I guess is pretty obvious and known to you...' Gautam added.

'You three can't take on 300? Let us face this...don't mind but we don't need your help and by the way thanks...' Mishti replied.

I felt like slapping her hard on her cheeks.

'Just shut up, do what you are told... don't use your brain which is of no use....' I shouted.

'Excuse me! Who the hell you think are you to order me?'

'Sorry!' I just put my head down.

'Don't be so bold or don't pretend to be strong. I know that no one can do anything but then also for a safe side... we will stay together from tomorrow and Mishti it is especially for you... so you just stay together...' Simmi advised her.

'Yes... daily we hear about the eve-teasing cases' remarked Kanika.

'Okay!' she agreed.

Few days passed and this all continued but as decided we stayed together always and then the day came of which I feared the most.

It was the first week of February and the maths class had just got over. I along with Gautam and Ambar was near the drinking water area when I received a call from Mishti. I don't know why but my guess was so accurate. She said in a much tensed voice, 'Where are you? Just come at the gate ASAP'

'Coming in 2 minutes' I replied and left while Gautam and Ambar were still drinking the water.

'What happened?' I asked.

She turned towards a boy and his group and asked them to speak.

'Hi! I am Govind and these are my friends...' he said.

'So?' I asked.

'Actually yaar it came to our knowledge that 2-3 guys were going to kind of propose your girlfriend... so it was not safe for her to go alone. We offered our company to her but she refused and we asked her to call you' he explained me the whole situation.

'Okay thanks dude!! But how'd you know about those guys?'

'They had once done the same with my girlfriend...I just heard them discussing something about Mishti yesterday'

'Okay thanks!!' I thanked him for his help and headed to van with Mishti along with those guys.

I had hardly walked 100 metres when 4-5 guys started approaching from a distance.

'These are the guys who are staring continuously' Mishti said.

I immediately instructed Mishti to go to the van and asked Govind if he could go along with her. She refused but then I insisted and said, 'Listen... I don't want any scene here...so just go...Govind and his friends will ensure your safety...just go. I'll be fine. It's you who they want not me...I'll manage...'

'But why are you waiting? I am not feeling good. Please come along...' she requested and a lot of care was hidden in those lines.

I refused, 'Let it get finished today'

She unwillingly headed to the main road where van always keeps waiting for us. I also walked slowly slowly and was very much frightened as I did not want to get smashed up. I increased my speed when one of them shouted, 'Hey wait...'

I stopped and then they encircled me, the second one and the main asked, 'Are you Kavya?' I replied with a yes when he asked again, 'Is Mishti your girlfriend?' I replied with a no this time.

'That is good...then you can easily provide us with her number?'

'Means?'

'Means...just give her number dude'.

'And if I refused?'

'Your wish brother.....' he kind of tried to threaten me. I thought and gave him my own number which had been deactivated over a year ago.

'Got it na? Now just go... and don't show yourself near her...stay away from my girl'

'Why?? Do you have any issues with that?' he tried to lean on me.

I pushed him a little and said, 'Just maintain a distance buddy and yes I have many issues with that'.

I don't know what he understood or heard but he didn't replied then, he just *slapped me hard!* I was not prepared for that slap and so I fell on the cycles parked behind me and one of the bicycles did the more damage than his slap! I stood up when he slapped me again and this time my specs were lost in the air. *Thankfully my eyesight is not so poor!!* I was completely overtaken by fear and I just raised my hand to get him off me when he slapped for the third time. This time his friends also joined him. One of his friends had some weapon kind of thing and that hit me very painfully on my face. The second friend of his found a long wooden branch of the tree that had fallen there some time; he picked that up and gave a deep blow on my head. This time I completely lost it. The impact was so deep that I lost consciousness for few seconds. I guessed that they approached me for this reason only, just to smash the *poor me*. It would not have made any difference if I would have refused to even start a conversation with them.

I was again on the ground for few minutes and got severely injured. He hit the final punch on my face and left me there. I somehow managed to get up and wiped the blood from various parts of my face and hands with my hankerchief. Ambar came few seconds later and was in shock and screamed, 'O-o-o-y-y-e-e, K-a-a-a-v-v-y-a-a…. who did this? I told you not to go alone, at least for few days…'

'S-h-a-a-a-a-t u-p-p-p. *D-a-g-a-a-b-a-a-a-z-z-z!!!* You l-e-e-e-f-f-f-t….m-m-e-e.' I said in a stammering voice as I was in deep pain. Actually it was fear not pain.

'Stop it… take him to the van and get the first aid. He is bleeding' Gautam overreacted. I was not bleeding that much. It was just a normal injury!

They both took me to the van where Mishti was waiting.

She just screamed and screamed, 'Oh god…What happened?'

Simmi and Kanika came and saw me in that condition. They also just screamed. 'I said it….I said it to stay away for few days… you'll definitely be the reason behind something like this….now are you happy?' Simmi shouted at Mishti.

'Just finish it…s-t-o-o-o-p-p-p-p, don't s-h-o-o-u-u-t a-a-t h-e-e-r-r…' I said.

'Idiot…stay quiet, uncle stop at any dispensary…' Ambar said to me and instructed uncle while he was wiping the blood from my face. My head was in his lap and I could see him laughing. He spoke, 'Are you happy now?? Had fun?? Hehehehe... you got beaten up without any reason... hahahaha!'

I smiled, 'A-A-A-A-H-H-H!'

'Stop it Ambar, and sorry Simmi and Kanika' Mishti said and held my hand. She asked Ambar to get up and let her do what he was doing. I was all painted red and my favourite white shirt was blood stained. She gently placed that hanky and more gently moved it on my face. She ensured that I do not get more pain but how do I tell her that all my pain vanished at the moment I kept my head in her lap.

I looked at her and saw her busy watching me, I smiled at her and she smiled back. I could see her wet eyes, maybe just because she was blaming herself for all this. I thought this for a while and then just closed my eyes because my fear of blood overcame my mental state but I could still sense her soft hands and her breath.

When I opened my eyes I was on the bed in my home and everyone had surrounded me as if I was the star of the evening. Then I discovered a bandage over my head and few stitches on my left arm and a bandage on both the wrists. I said, 'It's good that first aid was done when I was unconscious else I would have died screaming'.

'How did it happen?' Mummy asked. Now what to answer her, if I said 'that a bunch of morons did this to me then my coaching days were over', I thought but then Ambar answered, 'Nothing to worry aunty...just a small hurt in his head... he just fell from the stairs of the coaching' he saved me that day.

Mishti came closer and held my hands and said, 'I am sorry and take care' then turning towards mummy she asked, 'Aunty Can I stay with him tonight?' Before she could answer I answered her, 'No! Just go home along with others; I am perfectly all right'

'Okay! Then good night and take care, bye' everyone said and left.

I was worried to face Dad and soon he came and asked, 'What happened?'

I pretended as if I was in a deep sleep so he left but mummy narrated him the incident, I could hear that. The next morning Mishti called me and inquired about my status and was happy to know that I was better than the previous night. She then gave the mobile to her maasi to talk to me. She must have narrated her whole story. I said, 'Namastey aunty!!' she replied, *'Namastey beta!!* How are you now? She told me today when I saw her blood stained jeans'

'I am perfectly all right, can I talk to Mishti'

She handed over to Mishti and I asked, 'You told the truth to her? That I was taken down by the boys?'

'Yes, I also told this to mumma in lucknow'

*'Waah!!* Why don't you just get it published in the newspaper also? Ok bye...going for breakfast' I taunted her went for breakfast. There was a swelling in face and hands and movement was next to zero. I somehow managed to finish my breakfast and was completely taken away with fear when I remembered that I had to again go to that place (coaching). I was actually afraid of facing that guy again but next second I was thinking of Mishti. Her thought gave me a reason to go back. I thought, 'If she can go then I can also go...after all I'd taken her responsibility...so how could I leave her'

I should be thankful to that bad guy, it was because of him only that my dreams started to turn into reality, Mishti started to grow care for me and this time it was beyond the sense of friendship. She always used to be kind of more careful and extra kind, whether it was in the van, in the coaching or anywhere we went. She used to pay full attention to me and took proper care that I was safe and for that she avoided to spend time with me nearby that area. Every night she texted me, chatted for a long time just to ensure that I was alright and just to make me realise that she was always there with me. She always reminded me to take proper care of myself and it was due to this fact that I became more health conscious and took proper care of myself, whether it was the fact of taking medicines or taking proper rest.

For the next few days I used to borrow her shoulder whenever she sat next to me in the van and she always offered her shoulder, spent time with me, and sometimes also stayed at my home for few hours. I started to love her even more and could sense that somewhere within her heart, lived a part of me!!

During these days, she had inclined much towards me and I thought that she must have realised this but she never spoke of it. I firstly thought to start that proposal topic all over again as this time I saw a ray of hope, a silver lining but somehow stopped myself. I just continuously felt the joy of being under her soft care and stayed calm. I just left it to happen by itself and thought if it's meant to be then no power in this world can hinder its occurrence.

I just enjoyed a lot and with no fear attended the classes regularly both in the school as well as in the coaching. It was a quite surprise to me that I didn't see that guy again, I don't know why but he never showed himself, it seemed like this all was happening for a reason like someone above in the sky wanted us to be together and why not, after all I've prayed day and night for this to happen.

My first attempt met with a rejection, then that guy beat me and then Mishti had grown to care for me, all this was meant to happen, so that our destinies can come together. Just by thinking and manipulating these facts in my own way and for myself, gave me an immense pleasure, a pleasure that no other thing in this entire world can match with!

# Chapter Sixteen

I started recovering from my injuries, now swelling was all gone; I had a bandage on my head and on my left wrist only. The pain was no more but I felt it only during a headache or when hit again on the head. It was the week of lovers and we call it the very lovely and splendidly romantic, '*Valentine's Week*'.

Like always, like the daily schedule when I returned from school, I got a call and it was from Kshitij. I was happy to see his name on the caller screen as I had not met him or talked to him for a long time; if I could guess then I think from the day I joined coaching. I received his call and before I could greet him he bursted with anger, '*Kutte ho kya?* You got injured and then also you didn't tell... I got to know from your mother when I called at your landline... it's been around 5-to-6 months we haven't met...so today we'll be coming to your home...when do you return? Talk to Abhi and Sahil, they are with me.'

'Today I'll be back by 6-7 pm. Okay give the phone to Abhi'

'You must have told at least bro. Anyways how are you now?' asked Abhi.

'Better....okay I'll come tomorrow...at Sahil's place... what say?'

I guess the speaker was in and suddenly Sahil shouted, 'Not my home...don't forget the last incident... we'll be coming in the evening' he expressed his ultimate sorrow.

'Okay!!!See you in the evening then...bye'

'Bye... take care bro...' all three replied simultaneously.

I had just kept the mobile when it rang again and this time it was Mishti. I wondered why she would call now, when van was just to arrive. I received and said, 'Hi! What happened?'

'Nothing, can I not call without any work?' she answered, actually questioned me.

'Of course you can'

'Okay listen I actually called you to tell you that I am bunking the lecture today' she replied.

'Oh! Good good.'

'Arrey wait sir! I am bunking it with you my dear....' she said.

I was surprised. I didn't make any plan like this.

'With me?? But why?' I asked surprisingly.

'I've a solid reason and something I've to share with you...so please.' she requested and how could I put down her request and so I agreed.

Everyone went to the coaching and we went to the mall, although they knew that we were bunking yet we told them. None of them reacted differently as whenever anything related to me and her together is told, they always reacted in the same monotonic way.

Since it was near from the coaching, we covered the distance by foot itself. While on the way we talked, it was me to start the conversation, 'So what is the matter?'

'It is something very important...just be patient and walk slowly' she advised.

'Hmm.....so where are we going? She asked

'Japanese Garden' I answered.

We went to the auto stand and booked an auto, we didn't share it. The driver charged 80 rupees and dropped us there within 15 minutes. We entered the garden and as expected it was very peaceful in there and not many visitors were present. I remember well, I could hardly see around four-to-five pair of love birds and 2-3 families. We found an appropriate place to sit and talk. It was a little away from the main entrance and was situated in the centre of the garden. That place was covered with bushes and big trees. A big fountain was set up right in front of that place. The view from there was quite beautiful and it gave a sense of relaxation. The cool breeze kissed the face very gently and the promising weather added to the scene. The clouds made the sky to look like that it had been painted black, it was 4 pm and it appeared to be 6 or 7 pm. we could easily feel the fountain showering on us gently whenever the wind blew in our direction, and a sensation ran throughout the body whenever that happened. Above all these things, the best thing about the moment was that Mishti was sitting next to me and whenever the wind blew, it brought the sweet fragrance of her scent that was something rare to find on this Earth! I was thankful to her for giving me a break from the daily routine. That break was much needed.

Finally the moment was added with another pinch of beauty and that was her voice, it felt like someone from the heaven has just started to sing. She said, 'Very nice place! Good choice Kavya! This place is very beautiful and peaceful; I wish I could spend the whole day here!'

'Hmm so are you telling me for you brought me here?' I asked

'Wait...enjoy the scenario...okay let's take the rides' she insisted.

'No no no... no *jhuley*' I hesitated.

Those *jhuley* were not any ordinary ones, they were brilliantly built in various shapes, like in a shape of an elephant, in a shape of a shoe and many more. She insisted again so I agreed, I thought she would chose either the swings or sea saw or slides or those animal shaped slides so I agreed but when she expressed her wish, 'I want to go on that giant wheel....it is the real fun..Let's go', she scared everything out of me. I stood like a dumb.

I stammered and said, 'Do I look like a mad person? I am not going there, you know how much I am afraid of height and this is the biggest and largest giant wheel in whole city...i will not come along with you..' and I just turned around.

She pulled me towards her with her hand and said, 'Arey don't be a *darpok...* be a man...show some guts' and she purchased two tickets.

*They were not the tickets to the ride; they were the tickets to stupidity!!!!*

I unwillingly entered and got seated on the bottom most seat as if it will never attain that height. 'Sitting on the bottom most seats will not help you. They will also go up only...hehehehe. Duffer!' she said laughing at me.

'Hehehehe...don't try and act to be over smart, Just don't laugh...else I swear I'll kill you'

'Hehehe... Sure' she replied.

I don't know what happened all of the sudden and the whole wheel was populated in few seconds. *Saale abhi ye log door door tak nazar nahi aa rahe the aur ab achanak se aa gaye.*

I closed my eyes, and grabbed the handle and started whispering the *hanuman chalisa*. She laughed and said, 'What are you doing? Just chill yaar, okay hold my hand... and I promise all the fear will just vanish like...*saara darr choomantar ho jayega*'

Really for one second I forgot everything and just looked in her eyes, she just blinked her eyes as if she meant what she said.

I said, 'Oh! As if you are an angel' but I held her hand very tightly, it was half by itself and the remaining half by me......I then turned to the man in the control room and said, 'Bro...Don't give it much height please and also please maintain a slow speed'.

'Shut up!' she said and the very next second I was flying in the air and *I lost it when I discovered that along with the wheel, the seats were also revolving.*

It meant I was at the top most position of the wheel with totally in an inverted position, my head faced the ground and legs faced the sky. That time my heart was in my mouth and was trying to come out of it. It was really scary but I didn't open up my eyes for even a fraction of second and just kept shouting to stop it. I could hear all the screaming and Mishti was enjoying it, she shouted, 'Kavya open your eyes, the view is amazing from here, especially it's amazing to see the world in an inverted position.'

'Shut up...shut up...' I shouted back and just prayed to be landed safely. That controller kept the wheel in motion for 6-7 minutes and I guessed that he had done this purposely; he took more time than the usual.

Finally my foot felt some ground and I took a deep breath. We just went to the same old place where we were seated. I lay down and relaxed for few minutes.

'Did you enjoy? I did' she said.

'No, I didn't. Next time never ever ask me to do such a stupid and crazy thing. I don't want to get mad.'

'You are such a *darpok*. Are you a boy only?' she doubted me being a boy.

'Hehehehe...very funny. No, I am not a boy'

For the next few minutes we both just rested on the ground and calmly watched the sky without saying anything, the only voice that could be heard was that of the fountain. It just pleased the ears.

It was getting late so I asked, I asked for what we had come, 'Now please tell, what you were going to. It's getting late. We have to go back also. So, don't waste time. I also don't want to be the victim again' and laughed for a while.

'Nothing. I just wanted to bunk the class so I said this. I knew you would not come without any reason' she said.

'Just tell it at once else I am leaving' I said seriously this time and got up.

'Wait wait. Okay! I'll tell, come, be seated. Don't go please...' she requested.

'All right but only on the condition if you tell me what for what you brought both of us here.'

She nodded and took a sigh and finally spoke.

'Okay! Listen and I am damn serious. In the past few days I'd undergone the thought process over the topic that mainly dealt with you....' she said.

'Dealt with me??'

'Sshh ssshhhh.... don't speak in between, let me finish first, don't ruin my rhythm please and listen again. Yes, the topic deals with you. Actually from few days I am in a state of confusion, I am not able to decide or take any decision. I keep thinking of you and it had started since the day when you got injured. I know it may sound odd but I have kind of started to fall for you. I don't know still that whether it is love or what.... and since you are mainly involved in it so I thought of discussing it directly with you as you can only understand my state. I keep thinking of your proposal and it is not all of a sudden. That day I was just not ready so I had to put down your proposal, I will also not lie but I like you. May be now your feelings must have changed or whatever but I wanted to say this only. I can't predict about others but I know that you'll never forget me or leave me. There was so much love and truth in your eyes that day which I realised now. I am sorry for what I did. I love you!' she said this slowly and then stopped.

I was completely shocked. I could not believe what I heard that time. It was like I'd been waiting to hear this only. I thought now what to say, she had said everything and I had also expressed my feelings for her on the Christmas evening, but now what? She had stopped now and I had no words to reply her so what should I speak. There existed a complete silence for 5 minutes, she looked me, and I looked at her. We both were completely blank and ran out of words.

I didn't want to miss that golden chance so I had to speak, 'Actually the day you rejected my proposal, I was completely shattered but since then I'd managed to cope up with that stress and I hoped that someday you'll understand that it was nothing false. It was not your beauty that bowled me but your soul, mind and heart, I've already told you that. So is it a yes? And tell me one more thing that you said you gave it a second thought when those guys smashed me? It means that you were just waiting for me to get smashed and....' I could not complete my words when she pulled me closer towards herself, I just kept looking at her and the very next second my eyes were closed and something gentle and very soft touched my lips.

*Yes it was her lips!*

It was a soft yet comforting kiss. My heart beat rapidly in my chest as I realised what had just happened. I could hear her heartbeat too, it was racing with mine. Time stood still as our lips moved together sweetly making me forget how the time passed by. Her soft, warm lips tasted like strawberry. I could feel her smiling which made me smile too. I pulled away, my forehead leaning against hers. Sweetness matched sweetness. I was completely still, only my heart was involved in any kind of movement- beating. My both the hands were in air and eyes closed with a thought of what was happening at the moment.

She was really focused. She put her hands on the sides of my face to hold me. Then gradually she gained momentum and her hands were behind my head. Her fingers ran across my head, she slowly lost control of herself and took control of me, she started to lean over me and her soft kisses converted into the intense ones. Her soft lips were wet by now and I could still feel the warmth of her passionate kissing, I also supported her. It was the time when my both the hands which were in the air for so long, held her face gently and I tried to match her.

I know at sometime we would have to stop but I didn't want it, neither did she but we stopped after some time. She knew she was not supposed to that but she smiled genuinely making her already beautiful blue eyes, even more beautiful. *As always she made me go gaga over her smile!*

Her hair at that time was midnight black and flowed over her shoulders. I must admit that she had saccharine sweet lips and were blossom soft. I had never thought that bunking a class could be so much fun!

'So it was a YES, I guess?' I asked the stupid question just to save ourselves from the silence that was going to prevail between us if I had not asked this.

'Of course a yes, idiot!' she replied while partially blushing and partially smiling.

'Well!! That went great!!! It was the first kiss of my life' I remarked.

'Oh! As if it was my golden jubilee of kisses! *Huh!*' she got annoyed.

I looked at the watch, it showed 6:10. I said, 'Okay! Let's go now'.

'Yup!' she replied.

Thankfully we were on time, and not late. There was a different spark in our eyes, it was clearly visible but we tried not to let it appear. We just sat down normally and waited to reach the home ASAP.

I was happy for myself, after all whom I've loved so much was finally with me and moreover I was happy for the experience that I had that day, it was a WOW moment! I could not hide my joy. Kanika finally asked, 'What happened? You are looking very happy? Did she say yes?'

*Oh she got it!*

'No..... actually yes, she accepted it' I shouted out of joy.

'Oh! It's very nice. Okay so you know na what you have to do next? A party in the Pizza Hut!!'

The door bell rang and it was Kshitij and the company.

I was very happy to see them and also that day I was much happier, I hugged all of them and instead of inviting them inside the house, we went on a walk in the park in front of my house.

'*Aur mere laal kya haal?*' Abhi asked in his *shayaraana andaaz.*

'Improving very fast now...' I replied.

'Okay! You can say it' Sahil said.

'What?' I questioned him about what to say.

'Dude, we know you from childhood. When you have something big to speak only then your face glows like anything' he replied.

'Yes, he is absolutely right' Kshitij gave a support to Sahil's sentence.

'You all are dogs. Okay!' I replied them and started the whole narration, 'Actually I proposed a girl in my van. She rejected but today she accepted.... From today, I can say the famous quote that "*the lion fell in love with the lamb*"

'Congrats! When is the party?' Abhi congratulated me.

'It is really good to hear this' Kshitij said.

'Okay! Now just tell when are you arranging a meeting with our *bhabhijaan*? Sahil asked in a mischievous way.

'Oye! only *bhabhi* for you, *jaan to wo meri hai*' I corrected his question.

'Oh!' he said and ran after me to hit me.

'Don't test my patience Sahil. I am injured else I would have...' I could not complete my sentence when he grabbed me and said, 'Else what? Speaking a lot today. Kshitij, just catch him' he laughed.

After spending almost one hour with my *chuddhy buddies*, I bid them farewell with a promise to meet them soon and came inside the house smiling and then singing and again smiling. I forgot that dad was at home and he heard me singing *kaise samjhau tumhe mera pehla pehla pyaar hai ye.* He didn't say anything except, 'You, just come here at once'. Those words hit me like bombs. I went in his room and said, 'Yes'.

'Take the fees and hand it over to the driver of the van' he gave me the money and got busy in his work.

'Okay!' I said and thanked god, I thought he would have something else to say like a lecture on studies or on my health or whatever.

'*Aur zyaadaa pyaar na ho tumhe samajh aaya, aaram kar lo pehle*' he finally said it keeping his eyes on his papers.

I felt a little annoyed but then I went in my room to have a peaceful sleep. I waited for my cell to beep with her message but it didn't so finally I texted her, 'Good night dear...take care and I love you a lot <3'

'Dear? At least now use some pretty adjectives. Okay let me use it. You boys are good for nothing. Don't even know how to love...how to handle a gf... u should have texted like gn babu, or gn swthrt or something like this...you boys r just so unromantic yaar... okay!! Good night! My dear munchkin!! Swt drmzzz and tk cre... muuuaaahhh!! Lots of love... ☺☺<3' she texted back.

I wondered what the problem with her was. I thought of committing a suicide or doing something similar. I mean how mean she was but she was my girlfriend and now I'd to manage to handle her tantrums.

# Chapter Seventeen

From the very next day, the world appeared to be brand new, wrapped in sweet surprises and sky showered unlimited love upon me. My life of being a single was over, now I was committed and in a relationship and this life was far better than that single life. It was so lovely to wake up with a text in the mobile, 'good morning swthrt..have a great day... love you!!'.

A small message as that can make your whole day so beautiful, I'd never thought of it but now it felt great! It was all beyond perfection! Every morning brought a fresh energy with itself, an eagerness to meet your loved one and also brought impatience. I also started to focus on my studies well now, both in school and coaching. I have always thought that to be single is a gift but now I realised to have someone so special is not just only a gift but also a blessing from heaven! A fear always surrounded me but this fear was of losing her, there was something good related to this fear.... *I actually liked this fear...* Her image got imprinted on my mind, she was here, she was there, and she was everywhere! Only by thinking of her, I could find a peace in my mind.

After few days, it was 14<sup>th</sup> February, the day worshipped by the love birds and that year I also had a reason to enjoy. I also had my love bird with which I can capture the most wonderful moments of that day and cherish them later. That day I also decided to go public about our relationship (to tell in the van).

It was early in the morning while I was getting ready for the school. Meanwhile I thought that since it was a V-Day and so I'd to do something special, I decided to gift her something but could not make out, I Googled on my mobile but even then could not make out anything. I tried hard and then came up with an idea of the personalized gifts. While I was thinking about it, my mobile rang and it was Mishti. 'Hey' I said.

'What hey? Today is Valentine's Day and you didn't even wish me, you don't even remember, What kind of a boyfriend are you? So unromantic yaar...huh!' she started her series of allegations.

'Sorry, I was a little busy. By the way happy Valentine's Day to the first love of my life...' I wished her.

'First? What do you mean by first? It means you are hoping for the second and third love also?? You want someone else someday? Mind it, I am your first and the last...' she chided me well.

'I didn't mean that.. chillax!!' I comforted her.

*'Not a month has passed and she has started to fight over non sense topics' I thought.*

'Okay! Wish you the same dear...love you...bye....see you in the coaching...' she replied.

'Hmm....bye...' I replied.

It was the same boring day in the school except for the fact that Kanika had taken a leave; it was a V-day that day and so the atmosphere there was pretty romantic. In the corridor, in the classrooms, in the canteen, everywhere and every second some hearts broke into pieces while those who the lucky ones were, got the love of their lives. In that chaos, surprisingly, I met with two proposals... seriously I have never thought of it but I had to answer to two of them. It felt bad doing the most obvious- saying a *NO!!*

After I returned to the home, I was really shocked to see that my gift was ready. The credit goes to Kanika! She had a great sense of fashion, and designing, she really rescued me that day. All the day she had put in her valuable efforts to design it, actually she had made a big picture of Mishti by using small pictures of Mishti and Kavya! It appeared really great, and the brilliancy was that, the final picture just appeared to be like Mishti, especially her light blue eyes, but the tale ends not here. What was more fascinating was its gift box. It was more beautiful than the gift itself. I must admit that Kanika is a real genius and her ideas are incredibly exceptional! She had made a card of the actual size of that of the gift and pasted it in the card so that when Mishti will open it, all she could see would be her face in that collage of our pictures along with some *love quotes! That was a perfect masterpiece!*

'It is just awesome. Thanks sis. Everyone should have a sister like you' I said while buttering her a little.

'Okay! Don't be so much happy, I didn't do this for you. I just thought of trying a new thing' she replied as always and refused to take credits.

'That is the thing I was talking about, such a humble being you are! You always refuse to take credits. This always makes me cry' I laughed while wiping the false tears.

'Oh! Just shut up. It seems as if someone doesn't want this gift' she got annoyed and threatened.

'Okay!! Sorry and thanks...' I replied and took it from her and kept it safely in my bag so that I could hand it over to whom it belonged- Mishti.

While we were returning from the coaching, in the van, I thought that I would not get any better chance to announce our relationship so I took that out from my bag and with due respect and love gifted it to Mishti.

'Happy Valentine's Day....' I had just said that much when the whole little van echoed with 'O-H-H-H-H-H!!!!!!!! O-H-H-H-H-H!!!!! O-H-H-H-H-H!!!!!!!' They understood it and congratulated me and her.

'When and How?' Ambar asked.

'P-A-A-A-R-T-T-Y-' Simmi, as always, headed to her most favourite line. :p

'Shut...a-a-a-a-a-p-p-p-p!' I shouted, in the same tone.

'Just finish it guys!' I said and started to laugh slowly.

'Thank you...Seriously it is very beautiful, thanks a lot...' Mishti thanked me for the gift.

Then the photo shoot began, everyone present there treated us like a king and a queen.

'Click these celebs' Gautam said the right thing. Actually he was the first one to say something correct since we entered the van.

'Come closer...little more...' Ambar came down to his *chichorapanti!!*

After the photo session stopped, van also stopped and it was time to go.

It was the best Valentine's Day, not only for me, not only for Mishti but also for everyone present there and it was due to all of them, that we actually enjoyed a hell lot and special thanks to my dear sister!!

After an hour, she texted me saying thank you for the gift!

**Mishti:** Thanxx a lot dear... you made my day as special as it should be... just love you yaar... and the gift was super awesome... and the idea was very very cool and pretty!! <3 ☺

**Me:** Hehehehe!! Koi baat nahi yaar... ab toh aadaat dalni hogi iski tumhe bhi and mujhe bhi.....BTW your welcome.. ☺ but mera gift kahaa hai?

**Mishti:** Oops!!! I actually don't have it but tumhaare b'day pe interest kay sath dungi...hahahaha... tab tak kay liye isi se kaam chalao... muuuaaahhh!!!!

**Me:** Oh ho! Agar aisa gift milega tab toh kya baat hai... hehehe ;)

**Mishti:** hehehehehe!!!! Okay going to sleep... u 2 slp... gunnite...swt drmzzz and tk cre baby!!! Love you!!!

**Me:** Gunnyt Shona!!! Love you too... <3

**Mishti:** Oh ho!!! Shona?? Haa?? Not bad not bad... very lovely...I like it.. okay! gn...☺

**Me:** gn... ☺

Our Final exams seemed to have arrived early this year, it was like yesterday when I took admission in this new school and now it was going to be a year. Coachings were also closed for that period so that students could focus on their exams also and due to this I could not see her. During the exams, our talks got limited, we chatted very less. I thought that this might weaken our bond but cheers to us... nothing such happened! I thought that why should I worry as it was just a matter of about fifteen-to twenty-days and those days would easily pass by and so did they.

Coachings started again, but schools remained closed after the final examinations. I saw her again and it felt like I came back to life...it seemed like I hadn't seen her for years. She looked like the old Mishti but still appeared to be new. She was so full of energy as if she had been reborn. She looked extremely cheerful and charismatic! Days passed and passed, practically time was running and still everything was same, nothing has moved even by an inch! I was deeply in love that I could not make out when the calendar showed August.

I again overlooked it and thought about the journey with her that I have covered so far, it was such a soothing experience, like a ship sailing in a never ending ocean of love, like a rainbow always in the sky and that rainbow also had seven colours but they all were seven different shades of love- pink, red, and its shades. I thought about it and smiled and smiled and smiled.

Within past few months, my bond got more special with her. The colour of love between us became more dark with time and the understanding and tuning matched perfectly now! We spent as much as time together, we went on outings, or should be called as *dates?*

We went to movies, for shopping, and sometimes just *aiwai.*

The calendar showed 1$^{st}$ August and the clock showed 11 in the night when I got a call, it was as always Mishti.

'Hey' I greeted her.

'Hey' she replied.

'It's very late. Have any work?' I asked.

'Are you insane?' she questioned back.

'No! Why?'

'Idiot! It's the birthday of my babu, so I want to be the first person to wish you' she replied.

'Okay! Nice! But does it make any difference. Whether you wish at 12 or 12:15?'

'Yes, it does matter to me. You have any problem with that? And if you have then it is yours' she answered her own question.

'Okay! So tell me did you miss me?' I asked.

'We've just met 3 hours before but yup I miss you every moment dear... you tell...? Party?' she asked.

'Of course! Party but what about my gift?'

'I'll wrap myself in a cute pink wrapping paper. No gift can be more precious than this one' she answered.

'Oh ho! And what about the interest?'

'Interest?? What interest? She pretended that she doesn't know anything.

'Someone promised on valentine's day to return interest' I hinted her

'I remember'

'Its 12 now' she said.

'Yes, so wish na. What are you waiting for?'

'No, wait' she replied and after 5 minutes I heard a beautiful instrument, someone was playing the tune of the *birthday song*. I guess that instrument was a Piano. *Seriously girls and their ideas...hatsoff!!*

'*Offo!* Thanks a lot shona babu!!! Really a different way of wishing birthday'

Just then I could hear the waiting tune and unwillingly I had to say, 'Okay, now please let others also wish me. Will see you tomorrow. Bye'

'Okay! Sure...today is your day my hero. Birthday boy, go ahead and attend you calls...we'll meet tomorrow...good night...bye and love you a lot munchkin. *Ab Kanika ko wish karna hai muje...bye!!'* she replied.

*I still wonder what does MUNCHKIN meant.*

She then wished Kanika on her mobile as she shared her birthday with me. I also wished her and then after attending the calls from friends and relatives, I finally went to sleep. Kanika was still awake as her calls were not yet finished.

The next morning I woke up, took the blessings from mom and dad and went to take a shower. After I came out dad asked, 'Do you have money?'

'Hmm' was the reply from me and I went to dress up myself for the school.

When I picked my wallet, I found five notes of one thousand rupees. I was happy and shouted, 'Thanks dad!' I also found the same amount kept next to that of Kanika's wallet.

*Actually whenever I need money and when dad asks about it then I only reply him with a 'hmm' and he himself puts the money in my wallet but if I say 'Yes I have money' then it really means that I have the money!!*

Everyone greeted us as soon as we entered the van. 'Thank you' was the common reply from both of us. I expected that day to be special but it turned out to be even more special when we were returning back from the coaching. Actually it was all pre-planned and the master mind behind all that was Mishti. She has instructed everyone and explained well about their roles; even Kanika was involved, although she also had a birthday. It had been planned for both of us but Kanika knew about it and it was a surprise to me, that was the only difference, but it was for both of us.

As soon as I came out of the building, Ambar and Gautam escorted me to the Maggie point, as per the instructions. We just waited there and talked the rubbish about here and there. Ambar got a call from Mishti but that duffer actually failed half of her plan by saying, 'Yes Mishti? Everything ready?'

This gave me a hint of something but I could not guess it correctly as the surprise was very sweet and I had not expected that much from them. I headed towards the van when someone from behind closed my eyes and by the tender touch only, I could bet on it that she was none other than Mishti. She carefully took me to the van and slowly removed her hands but instructed not to open the eyes until said to do so. After a while, when I guess everyone was present, I was allowed to open my eyes and the first thing that I could see was a bright flame and when gradually I gained my full vision, I saw two beautiful cakes, one baked in the shape of the cartoons 'HUM' and 'TUM' from the movie *'Hum Tum'* and the other was of the cartoons BEN and GWEN from the famous cartoon series- BEN 10. They both looked exceptionally cute!

Like I said, *girls and their imaginative ideas!! Hats off again!!!*

As far as I could guess, that 'HUM TUM' was for me and Mishti and that 'BEN and GWEN' was for me and Kanika. So I'd to cut two cakes that night. Firstly, I took a picture of both the cakes and then first I cut the cake with my sweet sis.

Everyone sang and clapped, and then the dirty party began, the part I hated the most- PLAYING *HOLI* WITH THE CAKE. I became the victim, Kanika was safe!

Then I cut the cake with Mishti and this time the birthday song just got a better version, it was like- *happy*

*Valentine's Day to You!* Now this time I was safe and everyone else became a victim, *Y-i-p-p-p-e-e-e-e!!!!!!*

We partied hard at the famous *Kalyan-G bakery*. We again sat in our *pushpak vimaan!!!*

Mishti was next to me and then she took out the gift, and I was so sure that I hadn't seen anything so creative and beautiful. It was collage of her pictures but it was not any ordinary one! It contained a heart which was made after rearranging the different poses of her pics in which she had made different poses and had kept in mind that her hands also made various poses as it was the rearrangement of those hands only which made a proper heart. If someone focused on her face, then that person could see her different moods also. It was such a wonderful gift, **truly classy**!!

Behind it was a note written, which said, *'Through the months, I've shared so much with you, both bitter and sweet but it seemed to be like it'd been years. You've been such a comfort to me, helping me in every possible way. I wanna thank u for all those times u've brought a smile on my face, for sharing ups and downs with me. It's a blessing to have you in my life...every moment with you is magical....i must have a wish upon a lucky star to have someone as wonderful as you by my side..., I thank u once again for being in my life...together or apart, u'll always remain in my heart... on this day, what more can I wish for... but the very best for u...Feel special, feel unique!!! It's your day and on this special day...celebrate life..have fun...party hard... and listen to your heart... Just wishing you a very happy and a great birthday....and through this message I am just sending you the wishes to say to you that you blossom up the world around me!!! Wish you a very lovely and most wonderful birthday!!! May your day be wrapped in sweet surprises.... love you.... ☺*
  *-Always,*

*Mishti.....'*

WOW!! That was something romantic.....I had no words to thank her.... I was completely awestruck... I really loved her... I just gave her a small hug and said 'Thank you, this means a lot to me... Just tell me from where did you get these lines? Internet?'

She punched me gently and said, *'Dusht!! Hatt'*

She also presented a gift to Kanika, 'Kanika, this is from me and Simmi, exclusively for you Kanika' she turned towards me and emphasised on the last four words as if she was teasing me. I just laughed and ignored it.

Just then my mobile rang and this time it was Mummy calling. I received the call and said, 'What happened??'

'Your friends are here...Kshitij, Abhishek, Sahil, Lavanya, Himani... did you plan any party? She asked.

'No, I didn't. Okay! I think it will take 10-15 more minutes for me to come'

'Ask your van mates to come along, they are here with a cake' mummy instructed me, ordered me actually to come only with your van-mates else do not enter.

'Okay'

After few minutes we all were at my home, they first hesitated but then agreed. It was the first time when my school friends met my new friend circle. I introduced everyone to everyone, we again cut the cake, clicked as many photos as possible and then danced a little. I saw everyone was busy in the party, so I came out from the hall, went upstairs and called Mishti, 'Please come upstairs'.

'Wait' she replied.

'What happened?' she asked.

'Nothing. Where is my interest?'

'Oh God! You are still concerned about that interest?'

'Yes, so where is it?'

'Okay' she said and just kissed me, it was for the second time she kissed me but this kiss was quite a *sexy* one..she slowly approached me with a wicked smile and just dropped herself on my shoulders.....she first kissed on my cheeks... then she held my face and smiled at me and then gently kissed on my lips. This time I kissed her back with the same emotions and just matched her pace. Whenever she slowed down, I also slowed down and whenever she gained momentum, I also did the same.

The sequence of kisses turned into intense ones...I just pulled her closer by holding her back with one hand and the other hand was supporting her head. She looked unstoppable as she was so much involved in it. *For a while I opened my eyes and the only thing I saw was her cleavage!!* She just ran her fingers all over my head and this time my hands did complete justice with the lips, they first ran on her cheeks, then over her head, then at her back. I don't know why but my hands moved by themselves to her front and soon they were under her t-shirt. Slowly slowly running up! I guess she had not noticed about my hands as she was so passionately involved in the kissing. Unintentionally, it rested on her left breast and suddenly she pushed me back and shouted, 'No!' and then again continued with kissing. After few seconds my hand again rested at the same place and this time the result was much worse, she pushed me back and slapped me gently and shouted even louder, 'No! I said no...not now... You boys have only one thing in mind?'

'Hahahahah... Yes!!!' I laughed.

She kicked me and said, 'Shut up!!!' and pushed me.

'Now happy? Got your interest??'

'Very happy'

'Listen…stop joking now and be serious for some time, I also wanted to say something, and actually I want something' she said.

'Anything for you, what do you want?'

'I want you to make three promises to me'

'Promises! What promises?'

'See I'll not force you to accept any of those, okay! Promise number one is that never ever in your life you'll cry if I am not with you. I don't mean that I'll die or leave but if the circumstances are like that then….you'll move on with your life and never let it ruin or destruct you.'

'Have you totally lost it??? I am not listening this. I am going downstairs'

'See I am very serious. Understand?? Okay promise number 2 is that you'll agree to my all the promises and only then you'll have the right to love me'

'Shut up right now…..'

'Okay so you'll not agree?'

'Of course not'

'Okay then…it's over…every thing…is over'.

'Hey!! Wait….okay!! I'll agree, to hell with the promises, I can't afford to lose you but it is not a promise, it is a condition'

'Whatever it is….you have to agree with it…..so do you agree with promise number one??'

'I do, I'll never cry or whatever it is but I'll never let that happen'

'Okay… promise number two is that you'll never ever leave me. No matter what happens. Promise me that I'll be the last girl in your life and you'll never ever leave me alone in any circumstances. You'll always be there for me. You'll love me after death also and your love will never decay. As much as you love me today, the same you'll do 20 years from now. Promise me?'

'Okay...agreed...it's a promise....but what happened?? Is everything ok?'

'I am perfectly alright. Promise number three and the most important. Promise me that you'll always respect girls, women and also every human being...whether or not he is elder to you...you'll respect every animal...you'll thank everybody even for a little thing they did...no matter who he or she is...whether he is a street seller, a beggar, a vendor, hawker or anyone...you'll always thank them. You'll always respect girls and will stand for them'

'Okay baba!! Agreed. Now happy?'

'Hmm...I also promise to accept all the above promises..... and this is no joke... I mean it. I swear on god I mean it...'

This time she was actually serious.

'Yaar... I can promise one thing to you that I'll not lie to you....so I promise to agree with your proposed promises. I also mean it.... they are the promises which I'll never break...I love you and that's the only thing that matters to me'

'Okay!!' she smiled.

'I cannot even imagine the world where you don't exist so please never ever do this again...I love you very very much and I'll never ever choose to lose you!!' I said and somewhat became emotional.

'Are calm down baby... come give me a hug' she hugged me and said, 'I ain't going anywhere, always with you...now let's go down...'

After thinking for a while, I went down and soon everyone left.

It was really a special and the most beautiful birthday I ever celebrated. *Credit goes to Mishti and her promises! :p*

# Chapter Eighteen

It was the month of January, everything went very good so far, and we were going to celebrate the first anniversary of our relationship when she invited me to her home for the very first time. I was not nervous at all because I was kind of used to talking to her maasi but I had never talked to her maasa ji, actually he was also her chacha and her maasi was also her chachi! It is very complicated! So I was just a little bit nervous to meet him. The special thing about the meeting was that it was planned because her real brother named 'Gaurav' was going to pay her a visit from Lucknow. So she planned it in a way so that we can meet each other.

'Today you've to be at my place. Remember??' she asked.

'Yup, I do remember but I am very nervous'

'Just chill and relax...nothing to be afraid of...both of them are very sweet...and you'll tune up easily with *bhaiya*. I can bet...' she comforted me a little.

'Why so?? But what about your chacha maasa hehehe?'

'Shut up...don't make fun. *Bhaiya* is a car lover like you and secondly, I've told him a lot about you'

'Be on time...5 means 5' she reminded me of the time.

*I had really forgotten the time!!!*

'Okay!' I replied and actually I went to take a short nap.

Thankfully I woke up before time, accidentally though but before time.

I took a quick bath and dressed like a very gentle man, a full sleeve white designer shirt and all the buttons were buttoned, shirt was neatly tucked in and hair were properly combed, they were not like always like *bikhre bikhre*, a pair of dark blue denim jeans, wore my red frameless specs and stylish sneakers. I guess I never looked so smart ever before in my life!

I took the keys of the car. Dad was busy in his room so I told mummy, 'I am going t Mishti's home'

'Oh!' she teased me.

'Just don't tease. Where is Kanika?'

'She has gone to watch a movie with her friends. But why are you asking when you have to go alone?' she again teased me.

'Leave it. Bye...' I left.

As decided I gave a missed call to Mishti when I left, for what purpose was that miss call, it was a mystery. In the next few minutes, I was standing in front of her gate, I called her and asked her to come down as her pet dog looked like a demon, but in actual was he a demon or not, I don't know. She came down and escorted me to the drawing room where her brother was already waiting. After keenly observing the scenario, it appeared to me as if he was there to take my interview. I somehow sat on the sofa and greeted him, 'Hello bhaiya!!' and completed the *shake-hand ceremony!! Successfully!!*

I was replied with, 'Hi Kavya, heard a lot of you... so how's you?'

When he started talking, he sounded really sweet, I mean very friendly and frankly he asked me, 'Getting nervous?'

'Oh yes a little bit but I am fine. How about you??'

'I am also good. What about studies?'

I laughed and said, '*Dukhti rag pe haath rakh diya hai aapne',* took a pause and continued, 'Running smooth' that was the only answer to that question.

Mishti entered the room with some snacks and coffee. Her maasi also entered with her. Like a *sanskaari* boy, I immediately stood up and touched her maasi's feet and greeted her with a 'Namastay'.

'Namastay' maasi replied kindly.

After sometime maasi ji left and there were just me, bhaiya and Mishti in the room. Coffee had been finished a long time before so there was no chance of anyone saving us from the silence by saying, 'Coffee'. Finally I asked to save us from falling prey to the hands of silence, 'Is *Chahcha ji* not present?'

'He is doing some work. Should I call him??' bhaiya asked.

'No, let him do his work.'

I saw Mishti and bhaiya exchanging some gestures and meanwhile I observed him carefully. He had a well built physique and when I say a well built physique, then I actually mean it, it completely showed his hard work in the gym.... her short hair looked pretty cool and suited over him...long hair would not have done justice to his square type face cut, that was what I thought about his hair style! His veins were clearly visible from a distance and it completely gave a hint of his heavily muscular body. Since he was seated, so I could not made any guesses about his height but as far as

I can guess and by watching his body, any one can predict him to be taller than 6 feet. While I was observing him then suddenly he spoke, 'Listen, and let me get directly to the point. I know that you both are in a relationship. I only asked Mishti to invite you so that I could meet you once. I would not say anything, and I have no problem. I had complete faith on her choice' he said.

I just nodded and said, 'Well okay...it's cool...'

'Hmmm' he replied.

It was going to be an hour so I decided to leave and got up, bhaiya also got up and my guess was right, his height was at least 6 feet 3 inches, a real giant was he!

I was on the door when chacha ji showed himself unwillingly, I had just bent myself to touch his feet, when he stopped me in the half and said, 'No no, no formalities. Stay blessed' and he left.

Only Mishti came to see me off!

'By the way, you are looking very dashing today. White shirt suits you...okays...bye' she said.

As now it was our class 12th and Board examinations were upon our heads and pre-boards were going on so coachings were now over completely.

It was 6 January, her birthday but unfortunately we could not celebrate it as we have planned due to of pre-boards so I just wished her on the phone and in the evening visited her with some chocolate, stayed there for a short while and returned.

I texted her, 'Yaaar socha tha grand celebration karenge par kambhakht pre boards bhi...khair koi nahi..'

**Mishti:** hmm, koi nahi....u came..that was more than enough..it also made my birthday special...thanxx...

**Me:** hehehe...kk..chalo thik hai padho yaar tum..kon sa hai next exam??

**Mishti:** Physics ka...tumhara?

**Me:** oh!! Physics hi sabse hard subject hai pure 12<sup>th</sup> me... padho padho...good luck..mera English ka hai...ok bye.. love you mera babu!!! ☺<3

**Mishti:** hmm...tumhe bhi all the best... and love you always my munchkin...bye... <3 ☺

We both kept the mobile aside and concentrated on studies for the next few weeks.

# Chapter Nineteen

These exams time were not easy to handle. There was a lot of pressure, we had just finished our pre-board exams in the end of January and not even a month has passed when the final date sheet of the board exams was uploaded on the CBSE site, they were scheduled to start from 1st March, we had only the month of February left to prepare well for the forthcoming examinations. Students of the ISC board were to take the board examination from 25th February. I had a talk with Lavanya and Abhi in the past few days. They seemed to be equally tensed as I was. They had now stopped enjoying, they had not planned any outing, and they just focused on the exams. I liked their game-plan and strategy and was motivated to do the same. Although it was the first week of February, and the special thing about that was I had just completed the successful one year of my beautiful relationship but then also it lost its importance under the shadow of the board examinations.

I just texted her, 'Happy anniversary, my love...lots of love...hope this will never end...and I pray the same... ☺'

She replied the same, 'Oh! Thanxx and same to you, I also remembered it....and I wish the same for both of us... love you... muuuaaahhhh!!! ☺'

That's it, yes, that were the two messages that we exchanged within the last 20-25 days. We had not talked since our pre-boards or even if we did it was hardly a 1-2 minute talk. We had taken a decision to talk less so that studies don't get affected and our result remains good like that of the class tenth board examinations.

Actually our main plan was to score good in 12th so that if we fail to get admission through the competitions, about which we were more than sure, then in that case we could get a direct admission in any good university or college on the basis of percentage of class XII.

We were mainly focused on 12th because we want to take admission in a same college and admission through competition exams had a high probability of getting different colleges but this was not the reason that we had stopped studying for competitions, the main reason was, we had realised that we would not be able to crack IIT-JEE or AIEEE. Then UPTU remains and in that we can get admission in the same college on the basis of our performance of class 12th.

Every day I saw Kanika studying, which inspired me to study as well, although she was better than me in academics but then I also kept trying. I thought if not equal to her marks, then at least I can get marks somewhat near to her. She taught me whenever I had a doubt and I helped her when she faced any problem solving questions, especially the problems of Mathematics but I never showed her that I had a knowledge less as compared to hers. I always pretended as if I know more than her and she is just a dumb!

'Hey Kanika, help me out in solving this numerical' I asked for her help in solving the numerical of the subject that I hate the most- **PHYSICS.**

'See, here it is the question of a wave particle. The previous one was a point function. Read carefully' she advised me to be attentive when solving a problem.

'Okay! Thanks'

'Okay! Good' she said. I was going to leave the room when she said, in fact ordered, 'Give a water bottle'

'Okay...okay....' I replied and I opened the fridge and took the desired thing out when suddenly I saw the *SILK...* and shouted, 'You didn't tell me about this? Now forget it'

She came running to me and shouting, 'Just give it back to me, mummy ask him to return my silk'

'Why? Now who is calling mummy? Okay! Give half of it to me' I demanded my share.

'Okay!' she gave half of the chocolate to me, unwillingly though but she gave it to me.

We finally settled down and started to study in a full flow.

Boards came nearer and was that not enough when our admit cards of the IIT-JEE came, exam was to be held on 8th April and its centre was near to home. I immediately called Mishti and inquired her about the same.

'Hey!' she said.

'HI! How are you??'

'Fine. You tell'

'I am also fine. I just received my admit card of IIT-JEE'

'I also received it just now. So where is the centre?'

'It is some SLPSS Inter College in Kidwai Nagar'

'Mine is in RIS school in Ratanlal Nagar' she replied.

'Okay....cool'

'Where is the centre of Kanika?'

'It is in DPS Azad Nagar'

'WOW! DPS Azad Nagar!!! It is a palace yaar. I want to see that place' she expressed her sorrow of missing a chance to visit that actual school-cum-palace.

'It's okay! Better luck next time'

Finally the day came with a broad smile on its face, the first of March; the very first exam was of English. As mummy said, 'Do visit the temple-house' so we did the same...we also wanted to pray coz now *ab sab Raam bharose tha.*

I entered the examination hall and took the question paper, question paper seemed to be easy but it was continuously smiling wickedly at me as if it was trying to scare me. I somehow completed the exam and went back.

In the evening I texted Mishti to know about her exam, she replied that it was good, she did well. Next exam was after the gap of 3 days, I had plenty of time prepare.

Within no time I went to the examination hall to take my last exam on 22nd March, 2012. I very patiently finished it and looked here and there the hall. Excitement could be seen on everyone's face even on the face of the invigilators. They might be happy as now there boring 3 hours of duty were over.

I went home happily as among every exam, this was the only one in which I was sure to score above 95. In rest of the subjects I was not sure about the marks, exams went well but still I was not happy for the other subjects. I called Mishti to ask her about her exams, although after every exam either she called me or I did but then also I called her. I wanted to talk to her now as we were free, at least for a day or two!

'Hey! How it went?' she asked.

'Very good, yours?' I asked her.

'Same here. Okay! Listen, you and I are leaving for Lucknow in half an hour. You always wanted to meet my parents na? So today we will be going Lucknow'

'Are you asking or telling?' I confirmed first.

'I am telling you Mr. Kavya Srivastava that within half an hour you are coming at my home to pick me up and then we both are going to lucknow my dear.'

'Okay...let me first ask to mummy'

'Okay! But make it soon...'

'Mummy, I am going to Lucknow in half an hour along with Mishti' I directly told her, I didn't ask her.

'Ahem! Ahem!' Kanika pretended as if something got stuck in her throat and when I saw her she smiled.

'Will you come?' I asked, even though I didn't want that.

'No. I have some work'

'Have you gone mad? ' she didn't grant me permission.

'Let him go. Let him enjoy.' Kanika insisted on my behalf.

'Okay! But drive safely and slowly. Keep in mind that you are not going alone, Mishti is with you so drive properly' dad said, he had just entered when I was asking for the permission from mummy.

*Arey waah!! Ab to supreme court ki permission hai, high court jaaye tel lene!! I thought.*

'Permission granted, see you in 20 minutes...' I texted her.

'☺k' she replied.

As decided, I was on time to pick her from her home. She was late by 5 minute but I waited, and she was worth waiting for. That day she looked extra cute and sexy. She wore a black knee length skirt and a red shoulder crop top.

That day there was something different about her hairstyle also, I could not make it out but it was definitely something different.

Just then her maasi also came. It felt like and my first reaction after watching her was that all of a sudden the broad smile from my face just disappeared somewhere. At first I prayed *please god!* But then I realised that she came to see us off.

'Namastay aunty' I said and opened the door of the car.

'Be seated, drive slowly and safely' she advised to drive slowly.

'Ji aunty'

'Just you and me, alone!! Who'll save you now?'

'If I wanted to be safe, then why would I have come alone?' she asked in a sensuous way.

It took almost 35 minutes to come to the highway from the city.

'Half of the time is wasted here only. We'll reach after dusk' she expressed her worry.

'It will take only 50-60 minutes t reach there. Just chill!'

I was wrong, it became dark while we were still on the highway, and actually I was driving keeping the safety factor in mind so my speed was around 70-80 Kmph.

'I want to drive the car' she demanded to take control of the steering wheel!

'No, never...do you know driving? Moreover, it is dark now'

'Yes, I know a little bit of it. I drove in Lucknow and also I am getting bored'

'Then also, just stay quiet. There is a lot of difference in driving in a city and on a highway.' I said what dad used to tell me when I asked him the same question.

'Huh! Okay! Stop the car at some restaurant, I need to go to loo'

'Okay babu but why to stop at a restaurant? There are so many bushes around' I bursted into laughter.

She punched me hard on my shoulder and then hit me with her bag.

*That really hurt me!*

'You............just stop at any *dhaba* or something and now no more jokes.' She replied angrily.

'okay!...hehehe' I kept laughing.

After 5 kilometres, I found a decent restaurant and I pulled over, and I also went to the bathroom but I came before her. Meanwhile I purchased a packet of chewing gum and a biscuit. I had almost eaten more than half of the Hide 'n' Seek alone. She came and snatched that packet from me.... and said, 'You *Bhukhadd*. You ate it all alone?'

'I waited for you but you took much time'

'Shut up! Where's the car'

'At a distance'

'Okay! Let's go' she led me as if she knew where I had parked it. Then after few steps she stopped and said, 'Oops! Hehehe sorry!'

'Hmm...May I?' I asked

'Of course...please...' she said staring at me.

We entered the car and she finished the biscuits. I asked, 'Shall we move now? Still hungry?' I asked seriously but she thought that I was taunting her and so she reacted accordingly, 'Yes, please. As If I am the one who is always hungry. *Huh!*'

I looked at her; she was continuously staring out of the window and looked very beautiful when she raised her eyebrows.

'Who the hell are you waiting for?'

Instead of replying I kept looking at her and kept smiling. She then pushed me to and fro through my hand and I just grabbed her hands and kept looking at her, she became a little nervous and said, 'What?' I drew her closer and closer to me and we both can sense the warmth of the breath, I could hear her breathing deeply and also the voice of her heartbeats.

I just kept staring her beauty when she spoke in between, 'You are an idiot! One should not take this much time. Let me show you how quick it should be' and she kissed me. This kiss was the best until now.

She actually locked her lips with mine; I can smell that chocolaty smell of Hide 'n' Seek. Her lips tasted very chocolaty with a sweet tinge of a strawberry! At first she was slow, and then she outpaced me. Our tongues explored each other's mouth. We just got lost into each other for few minutes and this time it appeared to turn into sex! I kissed her with emotions and then I moved a little lower, I kissed on her neck, her shoulders and I dropped one of her sleeves off her shoulder and held her tightly from the back. My hand ran here and there all over her back and I could sense that she wore a *strapless bra!!* After I removed one of her sleeves, I continuously kissed her and again my hand explored the area under her top but this time she didn't stop me, I stopped by myself. I took a pause but then she pulled me back and this time she finished what she had started few minutes back. Seriously that was the best kiss ever!!

'Woah! That was the best one' I exclaimed.
'Hmm!! I also think the same'
'Are you wearing a *strapless bra?*? Hehehehe' I laughed.

'*Hawwww!* Very funny!!' she replied and pinched me just to save her from the embarrassment. She asked me to just drive.

I started to drive and she kept seated quietly for a while when again she demanded the same, 'I want to drive the car. Please'

I don't know what made me to do so but I agreed unwillingly and said, 'Okay! Giving it at my own risk but not more than 5 km and speed note more than 40. Okay?'

'Yup'

# Chapter Twenty

## *25th March 2012*

You woke up one morning and realised that nothing was same, and that what you would learn now will be even more horrifying!!

I woke up shouting and screaming.

Hearing my scream, a lady ran towards my room and asked, 'What happened son?'

I could not make out anything, I just replied, 'Where is Mishti?'

'We'll take you to her but for now, you just take rest'

'I know I met with an accident.....where is she? Is she alright?? Ya of course she is all right, I've just seen her a few minutes before. Will you please call her?' I answered my own question and requested her to do the needful.

'Wait...wait...wait...what did you just say?? You saw her?' she looked so troubled.

'Yes, she came along with you guys only'

I heard someone else coming to my room. It was the doctor, Mishti and her brother- Gaurav bhaiya.

'Oh! Here she comes'

'Where is she?' asked bhaiya looking furiously at me.

Before I could think of anything I turned towards that lady and asked, 'Are you her mother?'

'Yes son'

'Okay! I am really sorry. I could not recognize you'

She turned towards the doctor. The doctor nodded his head

'Okay! Listen beta....you met with an accident and a severe one. You were admitted in the same hospital in which Mishti is right now. Your recoveries were quite well so we brought you home'

'What!! Are you joking?? Mishti is standing next to you and has anyone informed my parents?'

'Yes. We have informed your parents...they are in the hospital. Mishti is in I.C.U' she tried to explain me.

'She is standing here in this room. Can't you people see her?' I was frustrated by then.

'Son, Relax! It is some concussion. You got hit at the same place for the second time. In this condition, we often see and hear those things which are actually very close to us. We only remember those persons, who were with us the last time when we were in conscious state. It is called *Hallucination!* It is just the set up of your mind. *It is not real my boy!*' the doctor explained that why I was able to see her.

'What!! How is this possible...?' I thought and closed my eyes again. I tried to concentrate hard on the accident, just to recall what actually happened that night and I could just remember that Mishti was driving the car and when it stopped after rolling, Mishti hit herself hard with the steering!! I opened my eyes and I could still see her sitting just next to me holding my hands. I just kept looking at her and said nothing, neither did she!

The doctor and everybody else left the place whispering something like, 'He is still in shock'.

I wondered what it could be but my head burst with pain so I tried to sleep for some time, I could still feel that Mishti was holding my hand. I thought that I was inching towards madness! *They said that Mishti is in I.C.U but I could see her.*

This all hinted that I would be mad soon!

I woke up after few hours and found mummy sitting next to me with her hand on my head. She asked, 'Are you feeling better now?'

I could not reply but I just cried and hugged her.

'You can't undo what you did…just recover soon. I should have never allowed you to come here' dad said.

'Stop it! We can't afford anything serious now' doctor interrupted in between.

I was totally blank as I could not understand what they all were talking about.

'What is he talking about?' I asked in a tensed tone.

'Nothing dear! You just sleep.' Aunty came running in the room and asked everyone to stop the conversation right there.

'I am going to the hospital. Gaurav is there from the evening' a man said and I guess it was Mishti's Dad. Yes he was him only!

'Hmm. We will also come and from there we'll go home.' Dad said and turning towards me he said, 'Take care…We'll come a day after tomorrow now'

Everyone left and I was alone in the room, I searched for Mishti but she had also left with the rest of them, I guessed so!!

The next morning I woke up early, actually I could not sleep even, I stepped down the stairs and explored the mansion, it was quite lavishly designed and I could make out that her parents were actually the rich people we just see in movies.

I kept searching for Mishti but I could not find her. I found Gaurav bhaiya talking to someone on the phone so I approached her and asked him about Mishti. 'Have you seen Mishti?' I asked.

He got angry and replied, 'Are you in your senses Kavya? Mishti is in I.C.U. You just come with me' he grabbed my hand very tightly and just took me with him to the hospital where only aunty was there.

'Gaurav! Why did you bring him here?' she asked in a shocking way.

'Enough mom! Now he must be told the truth'

He took me to the window and said, 'See, here she is. There is no Mishti in home you are the only reason she is here'

His words struck me like lightening. I was totally blank and completely shocked….words ran out…eyes became wet and body became cold.

'Stop it Gaurav. He is not be blamed' aunty said.

'Oh please! Mummy…he is only to be blamed…if anything happens to her, I'll never forgive him'

And then turning towards me he said with tears rolling down his cheeks, 'For your information Mr. Kavya Srivastava…you did very wrong…you just ruined everything' and he went out of the hospital.

I then went to aunty, held her hands and with tears in my eyes, I asked very calmly, 'Aunty I know, it is not the time but please tell me everything'

She looked up and started crying. I wiped her tears and asked her to tell me everything in detail.

'Okay! Listen then... what is the last thing you remember?' she asked me.

'I just remember that I and Mishti had just continued the journey from the restaurant, where we stopped for getting fresh and from there, Lucknow was hardly 20 kilometres. That is all I could remember'

'Okay! A passing biker saw the accident and told that a girl was driving the car above the safe speed limit. He also informed us about your accident and he was the one who helped you people to the hospital' she explained me the whole scene.

I just got on my knees and hid my face in my hands and I remembered the whole dam thing of allowing her to drive the car and allowing her to speed up. I was feeling very guilty about what I did. Somewhere within myself I was blaming me for what all happened just like bhaiya did. I thought that why I allowed her to drive, if I had not allowed her then might be this all should not have occurred or then she would not have got hurt as then I would have been on the driver's seat!

'This is the reason why Gaurav is upset with you. I am sure he'll understand. You don't blame yourself' she tried to comfort me.

'But Mishti??'

'Just have faith in god, son!! Doctors are trying their best. It is the third day of her in the I.C.U'

'I am sorry aunty…it all happened because of me' I wept like a baby.

'No!! Don't blame yourself please…' her Dad entered and he also comforted me.

'You both are our kids…we can't see you in the same position either…so just relax…' he added.

The doctor came out of the I.C.U and said something that just almost finished my world! *Pairo tale zameen khisakna* kise kehte hai, I understood that day.

He said, 'I am sorry but your daughter is in coma! I can't predict how long will she stay in coma'

He had yet not finished and the next what he said just stopped my heartbeat and everybody's else there, the ground beneath my feet escaped, 'One more thing, I am sorry to inform but according to the reports, she has also lost her vision, her ability to see…her head injury was very severe, it damaged her veins and now she will not be able to see!!'

Doctor looked equally sad as we were. Gaurav bhaiya shouted, 'No! Doctor do something please…. I beg of you… please…' he just cried and so did everyone.

He turned towards me, grabbed my collar and bursted. Anger was clearly visible in his eyes, 'See! What you did?? You just finished her life'

I stood there and said nothing, tears rolled down my cheeks and I had no answer to satisfy him. In just few seconds, my heart was loaded with a burden of guilt and pain.

'Shut up Gaurav! Leave him at once and control. It's not his fault…you wait outside' Uncle instructed him to behave. He also had watery eyes and he stumbled while speaking.

I just looked at each and every one there and it felt like I was responsible for every one's situation including Mishti.

Aunty just sat on the bench and kept crying. I waited and watched Mishti from the window and cried. I said sorry to her. I turned toward uncle and as soon as I touched him, he started to weep and said, 'Just never blame yourself for all this!!'

I nodded and asked him to see Mishti from close. He granted me permission. The door of the I.C.U was scaring me every time I looked at it but I had to open that door. It was scary not because there resided monsters but because there was someone for whom I've always wanted every joy of this world and now she was sleeping there. I washed my hands and took my shoes off and entered the I.C.U. My eyes were a reservoir of tears by then. Despite the cold temperature in the room, I was sweating out of fear as I was going to see something that I was afraid of. It was not Mishti whom I was afraid of but it was her condition that I was afraid of. Never in my worst nightmare, could I have imagined this. I cried and cried and went nearer. She was lying there very peacefully and was covered with a light blue sheet. I remained standing and observed her closely. Her injuries revealed what she had gone through. Her beautiful face was now a crash site. There were innumerable scars, some big, some small, some very deep and the depth of those scars was easily visible. A tube which appeared to be so monstrous for her pretty face ran down through her nose. Her glowing skin was bluish by the marks of several injections given to her just to ensure that she doesn't gives up! Multiple equipments surrounded her bed. A ventilator, a monitor to read her slow heart-beats, an oxygen cylinder and glucose bags and a blood bottle which was continuously supplying the blood through a tube which pierced her left arm. She had lost a lot of blood. I saw her small hand was dropping down the edge of her bed. I sat next to her, took her hand and placed it over mine. I could feel her fingers curling. I just kissed her hand and then on her forehead. I said sorry. I kept watching her and started crying, seeing my sweet little angel bearing that pain all alone. The pain I was having in watching her in the I.C.U was nothing in front of the pain she was going through on that bed with her eyes closed. I could sell my soul to bring her back from that painful condition but there was no one to buy my soul!

I was left there helplessly. I cried and unwillingly left at the call of the nurse who shouted, 'Please leave now.'

She was calling her merely a patient now! Suddenly she was a patient from my Mishti. My heart melted and it cried like anything.

I stepped out of the building to search for bhaiya and I found him sitting on the stairs. I sat next to him and joined my hands. I said sorry.

He looked at me and said, 'No need for all this, in fact I am sorry… I just overreacted… it's not your fault…' and he hugged me. I felt a little lighter.

'Can I ask you something?' he asked.

'Of course'

'Okay… I just want, in fact I beg you to please leave our world forever' he requested me to do something on which I would never agree.

'What?'

'Yes…you heard me. Listen I've no harsh feelings for you buddy. I just want you to leave and never return'

I was dumbstruck and unwillingly I agreed. A drop of tear fell down.

'And one more thing, promise me you'll just forget her and us. I don't want you to be with her now. I don't want that she should think that it was you because of whom she is blind. We'll tell her that you suffered a serious injury and have been recommended to some better hospital. Don't worry about her, we'll handle her. And you should keep this promise if you really love her! Just leave brother!'

'Okay! But can I see her for the last time?'

'No! I am sorry. Try to adjust your life'

'Please don't come in now…go to the home. Take your belongings and leave' he added.

I was all alone there… I stood up and left for the home.

I went down and asked him to come out. As he came out, I said, 'She will be the only girl whom I'll love till the end. And for her I'll agree to what you said… I'll leave but never ever let her miss me'

I waited for few hours in the hospital and thought about the decision I took. I wandered here and there and finally I had a discussion with the doctor. I handed him a page and requested him to keep it to himself only. I hired a taxi to the home. I just cried and cried and cried. I packed my bag and then and there left for Kanpur. Before leaving I kept the Xerox of the same page in Mishti's cupboard and left a note for aunty in her room which stated,

*'I am sorry to leave but don't think that I am leaving your daughter in her bad time. I'll never leave. I'll always be with her as a friend, as a guide, as a light, as her eyes. It's just I've promised someone, so I am leaving but then also I'll always stay with her.'*

Few lines got disturbed because of my tears falling down on them, but I guessed they were clear enough to be read and fair enough to be understood!

*The next morning I reached home and told everybody about Mishti being in coma and losing her ability to see. My*

*words were very painful; mummy slapped me hard and accused me of ruining a girl's life. For the first time dad slapped me. He also blamed me of the same reason. I started crying.'*

*She said, 'Don't cry…go inside…'*

*I narrated the whole story to Kanika and she was in shock. She comforted me and said, 'It is very serious…. but you have to be strong!' I just hugged her and slept while crying. Next day Ambar, Simmi, Gautam, Kshitij, Abhi, Sahil, Lavanya and yudy came to visit me, not all together but in a random sequence.*

*They all were also completely shocked to hear the bad news! But in the end it was just me alone who has to suffer the pains and guilt. They all just expressed their care for me and their sadness for Mishti. I knew they were not fake but I was not in a condition to speak to anyone, I just kept sitting, sometimes listening to them and sometimes not. I was lost in my own world! It appeared as if I was under depression and would go mad soon just because of the guilt!*

*Tears sometimes visited the eyes and sometimes just disappeared. I was stricken by depression and I could not appear for the IIT-JEE examination.*

*I could not also make it for the AIEEE examination, every exam was leaving behind and my mental state was still under depression. Then finally dad thought to consult a psychiatrist. Fortunately he proved to be of great help and he helped me out from the depression. But the pain was still present, I could not concentrate on the studies but somehow I gave my first entrance examination and that was of UP-SEE!*

*Kanika had taken every examination but unfortunately could not do well so UP-SEE was her last hope!*

*UP-SEE was the last examination and then I was free, just from the studies for a while, but there was no way out to get myself freed from the guilt that resides deep inside my heart!.*

*I used to remain in contact with Mishti's mother through telephone and she updated me about her health but her reply was always the same and that was she is still in coma! That sentence always stopped my heartbeats!*

*Few months after the results of class 12th were out and she scored well but they were of no use now as she could not take her examinations, she was still in coma! Every day and night I prayed for her but it appeared that my prayers were directly sent into God's spam box!!It was becoming hard every day to bear such amount of pain and to hear her being still in the same condition.*

*August came, and it was the time to join the college…I didn't want to join it as I felt that I snatched everything from her, her eyes, her chance to be an engineer, her world…and everything. I thought how I could join engineering when because of me she could not take her examinations….!!!*

*I felt sorry and there was nothing I could do, I wanted to see her but as I'd promised her brother, I could not see her but then I was reminded of the promise I made to Mishti that I'll never leave her alone under any circumstances. Every second Saturday I used to go to that hospital in Lucknow without telling my parents and hers! I always kept in mind that no one watched me, especially her brother!*

*I always just saw her from the window, cried and left after few hours!*

*May be this is the only reason that I am trying so hard to live the life!! May be she is the only reason…may be just by watching her gives me a reason to live…. gives my heart a reason to beat…. gives me a reason to fight!! May be just watching her gives me back my life!!*

# Chapter Twenty One

*March 26, 2013:*

It's not that my life at present is bad but it is not the same anymore. I am living my dream to be in an engineering college but there is something... something that wants to run back in time. Here life is a bit tricky, always stands up for a wicked laugh. It has become a bitter sweet symphony. It no more meets me with a hug, but with twists and turns. It has put more responsibilities on my shoulders. Along with happier memories there are a hundred concerns running parallel in my mind. Even today, the dreadful memories are fresh in my mind. Even today when I close my eyes, the slideshow begins. Now even the ultimate happiness has lost its worth. Without her I feel so alone. Tears have dried down and even they have left me alone. According to anyone's parameters, my life is running on track.

Of course it is!

But only I know the undercurrents running beneath this stillness.

Today I only wish to go back in time and erase that chapter from the book of my life.

I know that once the time has passed, it is forever, it cannot be turned back.

I am in college, it has been more than a year since that incident and I am still not able to recover myself from those frightful days of my life. If I could go back in time, I would just have erased that day from my life....so that Mishti would be with me now.

I miss her every day. I miss her every moment. I miss her every second of that every moment.

I have heard people talking about loneliness but let me tell you what actually this word means.

It is like being left amidst the beautiful journey by a person who promised who will never leave. You will be sitting all alone when you will be hit by a sweet memory of that person and you will just notice that you are actually crying. You will not be able to make out whether it is out of the joy of those memories or the pain of that someone gone.

You will lose faith in the almighty. You will search for that single person everywhere and you will never find her except in your memories. You will feel pain. Your heart will sob.

You will pretend as if nothing bothers you now. You will go around living a normal life but the pain will always hit you when you will least expect it. And suddenly, out of nowhere, you will be left dealing with a fresh wound all over again. You will keep yourself busy. You will wish death to smile upon you but even death will turn its face from you.

*Life will always be incomplete without you, no matter how complete I am. There will always be a missing part of my heart. And I am not sure where and how to find it! I am still finding path that will lead me to you. I will not say that take the first step and I will take the rest instead I will take all the steps that lead me towards you. I don't know what I should do to have you back. I am still searching for you in my endless search. Please have some mercy, God! Please re-bless me with my life..!!*

As promised to her brother, I never went to see her but as I had promised Mishti I still go to see her. Every second Saturday I go to Lucknow and still mine and her parents are unaware of it, only her Maasi knows about me going there, because she was the only other person(after her brother) who knew that we both loved each other! I must be thankful to her that she supports me...and believes me...!!

May be her family will also understand me someday, especially his brother who hates me to the core! May be that day, when she herself will tell him about my promises! May be that day will come when she will come out of coma, and may be that day will come soon!!

*Yes, she is still in coma! Every time my heart cried and sobbed and will do the same again until she recovers, till then I've to be patient, be calm, and just pray! I can only love her, that is the best medicine I can give her....until then I've to live under the burden of guilt and pain!*

But the thought of what will happen when she will come out of coma, just scares the devil out of me! Even today, eyes become wet when I think of her... how she will react when she will face the reality. How will I face her? How will I react and survive if she never wakes up from coma! Still this thought is crushing me from inside out and maybe I am alive to watch her die!

Now you might ask that why I didn't even when her brother asked me to…then my answer would be the same, 'It is not that I could not find someone else or something like that…it is as simple as that I didn't want to find someone else… I've loved her….it doesn't matter that she is blind or not….what matters is she, her love and her support….. I've not liked her, but I've loved her, I've promised her to be with her, always and not to leave her especially when she needs me the most….This was my *Promise of Love* which I guess, I have quite succeeded in *Keeping Alive!!'*

And as it is said that *'Love happens every so often' but TRUE love happens only once in a lifetime'*, so **MISHTI will be the first and the last girl of my life**…… *this was the another promise made to her which I will keep alive till the eternity…!!!!!!*

# Chapter Twenty Two

After reading his diary, Mishti was over taken with shock and only shock. Discovering the fact that she lost her eyes struck her as a lightening. She could not believe what she'd just read. She stood still.

She was completely dumbstruck! She could not decide how to react.

For few minutes, she thought hard but when she could not even decide what to think then she ran towards Kavya's mother.

'Aunty, please tell me the truth. It is becoming more and more complex now.'

'Okay, what you want to know?' she asked.

'Kavya has written that I lost my eyes too then how come I am able to see? Is it true, what he has written?' she asked impatiently.

'I will not lie to you but yes, Kavya has written absolutely true'

Her words just added to the mystery now.

'Then how can I see?' she shouted and cried at the top of his voice. 'Why don't you guys just tell me the damn truth?'

It was the time when Kanika and her father were also home. They all looked were completely blank. Kanika tried to take Mishti to her room.

'No, Kanika. Not now. Don't do this. I know there is something big that you guys are hiding from me. I want the truth' she shouted madly.

'Okay, okay. Calm down' Kanika's father replied.

He gained some courage and finally he told her the whole story.

'Look beta, don't panic and don't be sad. This will definitely break your heart. No more running away from it now. Be brave to listen it. It is true that you lost your eyes too in that accident and now you are able to see because someone donated the eyes to you.' He unfolded the mystery.

'Kavya? No, no god, no' she asked and at the same time prayed to god that it is not true.

'Yes' he added.

'B-b-b-b-u-u-t w-h-e-e-r-e i-i-s h-h-h-e-e?' she cried.

Now that was the hardest part to answer for the parents whose *son is dead!!*

As a man, his father has a hard heart or he has to possess a hard one.

'He is no more' he replied.

This was the sentence that brought time to stand still. She became cold. Her eyes remained open. Tears flowed non-stop. Her heart bled. She was in another world for few minutes when Kanika tapped her.

Mishti turned towards Kanika and tried to say something with her hands pointing towards Kavya's dad but her voice was inaudible. She just cried and cried and cried. Kanika hugged her but could not stop her. She stumbled.

After 4-5 hours when she was in a state to talk, Kavya's mother narrated her, the whole incident.

'He was in his car when he met with an accident. He died on spot. It took place around Holi this year. He seemed disturbed that day.'

Mishti just kept crying.

'We came to know by the doctor that he had signed up for the eye donation process. He had signed that after his death, his eyes must be donated to anyone in need.' Kavya's mother added

Mishti hugged her and cried for a long time. She sat in front of his photo and kept crying. She pulled his diary close to her heart and slept while crying. Seeing this, the whole family stood next to tears. Not a year had passed when they all were still reminded of him. Though it was an irreplaceable loss and even time cant heal them but they all were trying to be normal. They didn't want to see her like that as from now, she had his eyes. She had a part of their son now so they didn't want her to cry.

# Chapter Twenty Three

She had been lost since that day. She didn't want to speak to anyone. She just kept herself locked in her room and used to cry only. She hardly had a talk with anyone. She had a pending words assignment with her family now.

'Why didn't you people tell me about my eyes and Kavya?' she shouted and shouted.

'We were about to tell you but could not find the right time' replied her brother

'A-a-a-a-h-h-h!! For god sake, why don't you guys just s-h-a-a-a-t-t-t u-u-p-p. Don't tell me these idiotic reasons' she shouted again.

'You all must be thankful to Kavya. It is only because of him that I am able to see again and you all kept this from me? Why?' she cried again

'We are sorry, beta, but we thought you are still not ready to bear this harsh truth.' Her father replied.

'We thought that we'd lose you like we lost Kavya. We lost one child and didn't want to lose the other. He was more than a son to us. Please don't think that we are selfish' replied her mother.

'Yes, we know that he was very close to you. We love him equally. He had just given us something that cannot be paid back. Ever! Just for his sake, try and understand our condition.' His father added.

'Just put yourself in our shoes and then think again. We would have told you but at the right time. We are sorry' her mother cried.

Without answering anyone, Mishti left to her room and lay down on her bed.

Being mature and adults, they tried to handle the situation and they quite succeeded in it. Things began to run back on track. Life seemed to be normal now when one day she was reminded of that page which Kavya had mentioned in his diary. She jumped off her bed and ran towards her cupboard. She tried to find that paper and after a struggle of 20 minutes, she finally found that paper. They were two of them, one was a Xerox of the legal filled form of eye donation and one was a note attached to it.

*'Hi babu! If you will be reading this that means you have regained your eyesight. I just wanna say that I love you very much and I can't see you in this condition. I give up now. Even if you come out of coma, then also the pain and guilt that I have will never go. I hope that you recover soon. I have promised your mom that I will be your eyes from now and I will keep that promise. I may not be there with you but I will always be there in you. It is a hard decision but it should never be revealed to my family. Who knows, accidents happen by themselves or are created by someone? I am sorry that I could not keep all my promises alive but if you'll notice, then actually, I have kept them alive. I promised never to leave you, I kept that. I will always be with you as a guide, as your light, as your eyes.*

*I promised to love you and you only. I kept that also. I will never love anyone now. My life starts and ends with you only. I will keep my promises alive till eternity. I hope you recover soon. And for every time you miss me, just look into your heart for I am always there with you. Never signing off! Get well soon. Lots of love.'*

She completely broke down after reading that letter. She felt as if anyone had stabbed her. She felt cheated. Now she realised that Kavya planned this way before his accident took place. She understood that it was not an accident; in fact, he drove to accident so that it may look like it. Now she had her every single answer. What he did was to donate his eyes as in India it is not legal to donate eyes before death. She sat there helplessly and blamed herself for her loss. Her eyes dried out of crying. She pulled his diary close to herself and cried even though tears ran out. All his memories flashed across her face. She became numb. She lost control over her tears and finally the dried eyes flowed with tears. Her heart seemed to stop beating. She sat motionless in front of his photo, just staring at that wid her widened eyes. It appeared as if she was talking to Kavya, silently. She was unrest. There was complete silence in her room. The only voice that could be heard was of the fan revolving. She sat there helplessly. Tears flowed nonstop and her eyes remained open. She resisted any movement. It appeared as if her soul had left her body. She cried, cried and cried.

# Epilogue

I don't know what happened to her then. Was she able to recover from such a disaster? Was she again in the old condition? Was she also dead soon? Did that step ruin her life? Had that decision for the betterment proved fatal? Was love at fault? Was it a fault? Was it that love became weak? Were the promises of love kept alive? These questions have no answers. Neither I have the answers nor you have but one thing that I know is that-

As long as she lived or as long as she will be alive, she will have no reason to smile. There will be no moment now that could make her lively again. She will be normal, she will pretend to enjoy, she will talk but she will always miss him. She will live only by his memories. His memories, his love will give her the daily courage which she will need to struggle with her life every day. His love will be her medicine now and it will only give her the reason to wear a fake smile as Kavya had always loved her smile. He always said, 'He would die to see her smiling'

Unfortunately, he proved it right!

He forgot the fact that the loss of loved ones leaves a vacuum in one's life that can never be filled. Ever!

It was what Kavya wanted, a lifelong happiness for her but did he succeed in providing that? Was he able to keep the Promise of Love alive?